SURRENDERED HEARTS
VERMONT BLESSINGS SERIES - BOOK TWO

CARRIE TURANSKY

FLOWING STREAM BOOKS

Surrendered Hearts
Copyright Carrie Turansky 2021
Published by Flowing Stream Books
Lawrenceville, New Jersey 08648
ISBN 978-7335292-8-0
Cover design by Carrie Turansky
Photo by Andrew Welch on Unsplash

All rights reserved. Except for use in any review, the reproduction or utilization of this work in whole or in part in any form by any electronic, mechanical or other means, now known or hereafter invented, including xerography, photocopying and recording, or in any information storage or retrieval system, is forbidden without permission of the editorial office, Flowing Stream Books, Lawrenceville, NJ 08648.

❦ Created with Vellum

*This book is dedicated to my daughters:
Melissa, Elizabeth, and Megan.
Each of you is beautiful in my eyes and in the eyes of the One who created you!*

∼

*"Teach me your way, O LORD, and I will walk in your truth;
give me an undivided heart, that I may fear your name. I will praise you, O Lord my God,
with all my heart; I will glorify your name forever. For great is your love toward me;
you have delivered me from the depths of the grave.
Psalm 86: 11 – 13 NIV*

BOOKS BY CARRIE TURANSKY

The Edwardian Bride Series, English Historical Romance
The Governess of Highland Hall (Book one) 2013
The Daughter of Highland Hall (Book two) 2014
A Refuge at Highland Hall (Book three) 2015

The McAllister Family Novels, English and Canadian Historical
No Ocean Too Wide (Book one) 2019
No Journey Too Far (Book two) 2021

Stand-Alone English Historical Romance
Shine Like the Dawn, 2017
Across the Blue, 2018

Vermont Blessings Series, Contemporary Inspirational Romance
Along Came Love, (Book one) 2021
Surrendered Hearts (Book two) 2021

Bayside Treasures Series, Contemporary Inspirational Romance
Seeking His Love (Book one) 2019
A Man to Trust (Book two) 2019
Snowflake Sweethearts (Book three) 2019

Contemporary Novellas
Moonlight Over Manhattan, (e-book only) 2016
Where Two Hearts Meet (Two-novella collection, including *Tea for Two* and *Wherever Love Takes Us,* previously published in Kiss the Cook and Wedded Bliss) 2014

Historical Novellas and Novella Collections

Waiting for His Return (eBook only, previously titled *A Shelter in the Storm* in A Blue and Gray Christmas) 2017

Mountain Christmas Brides (Nine-novella collection, including *A Trusting Heart* which was previously published in Christmas Mail-Order Brides) 2016

A Joyful Christmas (Six-novella collection, including *A Shelter in the Storm*, which was previously published in A Blue and Gray Christmas and as Waiting for His Return) 2020

ABOUT THE AUTHOR

Carrie Turansky is the award-winning author of more than twenty inspirational novels and novellas and a winner of the ACFW Carol Award, the International Digital Award, and the Holt Medallion. She loved traveling to England to research her latest Edwardian novels including No Journey Too Far, Ocean Too Wide, Across the Blue, and The Highland Hall series. Her novels have received stared reviews from Christianbooks.com and Library Journal. They have been translated into several languages and enjoyed by readers around the world. Connect with Carrie on her website: http://carrieturansky.com, and on Facebook, Instagram, and Pinterest.

facebook.com/authorcarrieturansky
twitter.com/carrieturansky
instagram.com/carrieturansky

CHAPTER 1

A wisp of smoke curled through the tall evergreens and drifted toward Jennifer Evans like a ghostly snake. Her steps stalled, and she clutched the handle of her duffle bag until her nails bit into the palm of her hand. The scent of burning wood filled her nose. Her throat tightened, and her heart raced as if some primitive survival instinct had kicked in.

Stop! It's just smoke from a fireplace or wood stove. She inhaled a calming breath and forced her frightening memories back into their hiding place.

Shifting her focus away from the trees, she searched the quiet Vermont road ahead of her. The man at Wild River Resort said it was only about a mile to her brother's house. But the weight of the duffle bag pulling on her tender right arm made her feel like she'd already walked twice that far.

She could see why her brother liked Vermont. Birds darted through the trees, calling to each other. A slight breeze lifted the evergreen branches in a swaying dance. The refreshing scent of pine and cedar replaced the offensive smoky odor.

It was wild, beautiful, and peaceful. Her heart ached at that thought. Peace seemed like a dream she could never quite grasp no matter how hard she tried, and the turmoil of the last few months had only heightened the needs in her heart.

Sighing, she shook her head. She had to find her brother. Switching her bag to the other hand, she started off again.

The road curved to the right and she spotted a house set back under the shady trees. Number 427 was painted on the mailbox. That was it. A tremor passed through her fingers as she reached in her jeans pocket and pulled out the folded letter from Wes inviting her to his wedding. She checked the return address. His scratchy, almost illegible handwriting brought a small smile to her lips. He should have been a doctor instead of a missionary, she mused. Then she reminded herself he wasn't a missionary anymore. Now he worked as an assistant naturalist at the Wild River Resort Nature Center.

She tucked the letter back in her pocket. How would he feel about her arriving a few weeks early for his wedding?

Lifting her gaze, she studied her brother's two-story house. It looked more like a summer cabin with the outside walls covered in cedar shakes washed soft gray in the late morning sunlight. Wildflowers and untrimmed grasses filled the front yard except for the area around a neat stone path that led to a modest porch and a front door painted dark green. Two large wooden bird feeders hung from a tree near one of the windows, and a shiny new black pickup sat in the gravel driveway.

Not bad for an ex-missionary. Her brother must be doing better than she'd imagined.

She studied the small house again, doubt stirring her stomach into a nervous stew. What if he didn't have an extra bedroom, or he was uncomfortable with the idea of her staying until the wedding? She didn't need her own room. She could sleep on a couch or the floor if she had to. With less than eighty dollars in her pocket and everything she owned in her duffle bag, she didn't have too many options.

She tugged at her long-sleeved shirt, checking to be sure the cuffs and top button were securely fastened, then followed the path to the house. With one more curious glance at the new truck, she climbed the three steps to the porch and knocked on the door.

It had been almost three years since she'd seen her brother. He was five years older, so they'd drifted apart after he left for college. But their disagreements about faith had created the largest gap between them.

She knocked again and studied the silent door. A warm breeze lifted her long blond hair, and she tucked it behind her ears. Uneasiness tightened her chest as she rapped loudly a third time.

The door creaked open about a foot. A sleepy-eyed man, who was definitely not her brother, squinted out at her. "Can I help you?"

She sucked in a startled gasp. "I'm sorry. I thought this was 427 Shelton Road."

He rubbed the dark bristles on his square chin. "It is. What can I do for you?"

Confusion stole her words as she looked at him. He seemed to be about the same age as her brother, but he was leaner and a bit taller. His dark-brown, wavy hair brushed the back collar of his rumpled t-shirt, and the baggy, green plaid flannel pants he wore made it look as though he'd just climbed out of bed.

"I'm looking for my brother, Wes Evans," she finally managed to croak.

His blue-gray eyes widened, and a slow smile lit up his face. "Jennifer?"

She nodded, her mind spinning. Did she know him?

He laughed and looked her up and down with a bold grin. "Wow, you look so different, I didn't recognize you."

Heat flashed up her neck, and she clutched the collar of her shirt closed.

His dark brows dipped, his smile fading. "I'm sorry. I'm Bill Morgan, Wes's roommate. We met when you came out for his college graduation."

Biting her lip, she tried to recapture the foggy memory of the event she'd attended seven years earlier. She'd met several of Wes's friends, but she'd been only seventeen at the time. She'd felt totally out of place and couldn't recall any of their names or faces now.

He waved his hand, dismissing her poor memory with a chuckle. "It's okay. Don't worry, I won't take it personally. That was a long time ago, and I'm sure I looked different in a cap and gown."

"Is my brother here?" She leaned slightly to the right and tried to catch a glimpse past his shoulder.

"No, he's probably over at Lauren's. But come in. I'll give him a call." Bill stood back and held the door open for her. He cocked his head and assessed her again. "Did he know you were coming today?"

She hesitated on the threshold. "Well . . . he invited me for the wedding."

Bill lifted his dark eyebrows, questions reflected in his blue eyes. "The wedding. Right. Well, I'm sure he'll be glad to see you."

She hoisted her duffle bag higher and tried to look confident as she followed him inside. They passed a small bathroom on the right and then a bedroom or den with a couch, computer, and overflowing bookshelves. A large map hung on the wall opposite the open door along with framed photos of a stunning sunset and another of a rocky coastline and lighthouse.

As they moved into the kitchen, Bill stopped and turned to her. "I didn't see a car. How did you get here?"

Discomfort prickled through her, but she straightened and

looked him in the eye. "I took an overnight flight from Portland, Oregon to Boston, then I caught a bus to Wild River. I thought I'd find Wes at the Nature Center, but it's closed today, so the man at the desk in the lodge gave me directions here."

"You walked from the lodge?" Frowning, he crossed his arms.

She nodded and felt her confidence melt away under his penetrating gaze. Though her desperate financial situation wasn't totally her fault, she still felt embarrassed by it.

His expressions softened. "That's a long trip." He reached for her duffle bag. "Let me put your bag over here for now." He set it on the floor by the couch where the kitchen and dining area connected with the living room. "Why don't you sit down, and I'll give Lauren a call and see if I can track down Wes."

He motioned toward the couch, but she walked to the sliding glass door that overlooked the back yard, hoping for a moment to collect her thoughts.

The house looked larger than she'd first believed, but she doubted Wes would want her to stay. He had a roommate, and it would probably be an imposition on both of them.

This was a mistake. She shouldn't have come.

Tears blurred her vision as she stared at the quiet forest and stone path leading downhill to a small stream. Yellow and white wildflowers peeked out around the rocks lining the walkway. It was a beautiful spot—the perfect place for her to rest and recover while she made plans for a new life she couldn't begin to imagine.

She heard Bill walk away and shut a door. The sound of his voice carried through the wall. His words were unclear, but she could hear the whispered intensity of his voice. Her arrival had obviously caught him by surprise, and though he pretended to be friendly, she could tell he didn't want her to stay. Why should he? He didn't know her. To him she was probably an irritation and a nuisance.

∿

BILL CLICKED the hair dryer on high and pointed it at the steamy bathroom mirror. He had heard Wes's car pull in the gravel driveway before he climbed in the shower about ten minutes ago. Hopefully that had given Wes and his sister time for a private reunion.

The dryer cleared a large circle, and he checked his reflection. Wow, three days with the flu had left him looking pale and haggard. No wonder Jennifer had been so startled when he'd opened the door. She had no idea he'd been sick and probably thought he was a lazy guy who stayed in bed until noon every day. He blew out deep breath. Well, it wouldn't be the first time a woman had misunderstood him, and it wouldn't be the last.

He frowned at the mirror. He definitely needed a shave. A haircut wouldn't hurt either. He combed his wet hair back and turned to check the view from the left and right. This longer look wasn't so bad. Maybe he'd leave it this way.

Groaning, he shook his head. What was the matter with him? He didn't usually spend more than a couple minutes in front of the mirror each morning, but Jennifer's arrival had thrown him for a loop. And he had a feeling his roommate was going to be surprised too.

Wes and Lauren's wedding wasn't scheduled until mid-August, more than two months away. Did Jennifer expect to stay with them all summer? He grabbed the can of shaving cream and squirted some in his hand.

Sharing his house with Wes had worked out fine. But where would they put Jennifer? He had three bedrooms, but he used the third as an office, and he'd already shifted a lot of his belongings to the attic to make room for Wes in the second bedroom upstairs. It wouldn't work. The house was too small for a third person.

Guilt hit him hard. His name might be on the title, but this house belonged to the Lord. That commitment had prompted him to invite Wes to move in after he had been released from prison in the Middle East for his undercover missionary work.

If Jennifer needed a place to stay, he should be willing to do the same for her. But the idea of a woman living under his roof, especially an attractive woman like Jennifer, didn't seem right.

The memory of another woman with long, honey-blond hair and haunting hazel eyes too much like Jennifer's flooded his memory.

He glared in the mirror, disgusted with the path his thoughts had taken. Get over it! Kelsey Moore was not the one for you and neither is Jennifer Evans. Let it go. You've got a good life with your work and church and friends. You don't need that kind of trouble.

He pulled a clean navy-blue t-shirt over his head and checked the mirror once more. It looked like he'd lost a few pounds since he'd been sick, but at least his stomach wasn't giving him fits today. It felt good to be hungry again. He could probably put away a big plate of scrambled eggs and toast with no trouble at all.

He'd whip up some long overdue breakfast and have a talk with Wes. Jennifer could stay for a few days. A week or two tops. Then she'd have to go. No way was he opening his home or heart to someone like her.

CHAPTER 2

Bill walked into the kitchen, and his gaze shifted to the sliding glass door. Wes stood silhouetted by the mid-day sunlight, holding his sister in a tight embrace. The top of Jennifer's head didn't even reach Wes's shoulder, making her look small and vulnerable. Tears slid down her cheeks as she clung to her brother.

Bill stopped in the doorway, taken aback by the scene.

Wes swayed slightly as he patted Jennifer's back. "Hey, it's okay to cry. You've been through a lot."

"I feel like such an idiot," she mumbled then sniffed.

"No. It's not your fault." Wes leaned back to look into her face.

"But I didn't have any renter's insurance."

Wes sent her an understanding look. "I know how hard it is to lose everything. When I was arrested, they took my computer, everything in my apartment, and my car. I even had to wear borrowed clothes when I was finally released."

"Oh, Wes, I still can't believe that happened to you. And all you were trying to do was help people." Jennifer's voice sounded shaky, but at least she'd stopped crying.

"It's okay. Possessions can be replaced. I still have what

counts—my faith and my friends." He turned slightly and nodded to Bill, a look of appreciation in his eyes.

Bill tucked his hands in his jeans pockets. "Sorry, I didn't mean to interrupt."

"It's okay." Wes let go of Jennifer and took a step back.

"I was just going to make coffee," Bill said. "Would you like some?"

Jennifer sent him a hesitant glance and shook her head.

"Not right now, but you go ahead," Wes said.

Bill took out the coffee, pondering the bond between Wes and his sister. It stirred a strange longing in him. He'd often wondered what it would be like to have a brother or sister who would always be there, someone connected by family ties that couldn't be broken.

These last few months, working with Wes at the Nature Center and sharing the house, had filled a void in Bill's life and reminded him of the benefits of deep and lasting friendships. But when summer was over, Wes would marry Lauren and move to Long Meadow. Bill would be on his own again. He pushed that uncomfortable thought away.

Jennifer exhaled a shuddering breath. "Everyone says I should think positive and be thankful I'm alive. I don't really care about all my stuff, but losing Beau has been. . ."

"I know." Wes grabbed a few tissues from a box on the end table and handed them to her. "And you need time to grieve all those losses."

Bill poured water into the coffeemaker, feeling like a first-class heel for his selfish thoughts about sending Jennifer packing. Though he wasn't clear on the details, she was obviously going through a tough time.

"If I'd known what happened, I'd have been on the first plane to Portland." Emotion thickened Wes's voice. "But you're here now. That's what matters." He slipped his arm around his sister's shoulder and kissed the top of her head.

She smiled up at him through misty eyes. "Thanks, Wes."

His eyes glistened as Jennifer reached to hug him again. He held her for a moment then cleared his throat. "You must be tired. Why don't you lie down in my room for a while? We can talk more when you get up." He walked over to pick up her duffle bag. "Come on. I'll show you the way."

"Okay." She sent Bill another uncertain glance as she followed her brother toward the stairs.

Was she uncomfortable because he'd seen her tears or because she knew her unannounced visit put him in an awkward position? Bill mulled those questions over as he watched the coffee drip. When it finally finished, he filled his mug and added cream and sugar. As he took a sip, he considered the look of relief on Jennifer's face the moment Wes told her she could rest in his room. She was obviously exhausted. Why hadn't he thought of that?

Wes returned to the kitchen. "That coffee smells good." He pulled out a dark green mug with the Wild River Resort motto stamped in gold on the side and poured a steaming cup.

Bill took a carton of eggs from the fridge. "Did you know she was coming today?"

Wes shook his head. "I called her in March to tell her Lauren and I were engaged, but her phone was disconnected. So, I sent her a letter and invited her to come out for the wedding."

Bill nodded. That still didn't explain why she'd arrived in early June for a wedding that wasn't scheduled until August. He pulled the frying pan from the cabinet.

Wes leaned back against the counter and crossed his arms. "Is it okay with you if she stays with us for a while?"

"Sure. It's fine." Bill cracked an egg into the bowl.

Wes continued watching him. "What's the matter?"

"I guess it would've been nice if you'd have asked me first, before you invited her out here."

A puzzled look settled on his friend's face. "I wasn't

expecting her to come now, but under the circumstances it makes sense."

"What do you mean?"

"Sorry. I guess you didn't hear the first part of her story."

"Nope." Bill grabbed a fork from the drawer and stirred his eggs.

"There was an explosion and fire at her apartment in Portland. She lost everything."

Bill's hand stilled. "How'd that happen?"

"A construction company cut a gas line. She smelled it and went outside to check things out. The guy she talked to claimed it wasn't dangerous. He was even smoking." Wes shook his head, frustration lining his face. "When she walked back toward her apartment, the whole back wall exploded and crashed in. Debris fell all around her, but her only thought was getting back inside to rescue her dog."

Bill dropped the wire whisk, splattering the egg mixture. "She went back in the apartment after the explosion?" He grabbed a sponge and swiped the counter.

"Yeah. She ran around to the front and went in that way. She couldn't find her dog, but she wouldn't give up. She finally passed out from breathing all the smoke. A fireman found her and carried her out."

Bill tried to swallow away the burning sensation rising in his throat. Here he was worried about the inconvenience of sharing his house, and she'd almost died in a fire. "Sorry. I had no idea." He shook his head. "Man, she must've really loved that dog."

"Yeah, she's always been a real animal lover. And since our parents are gone, and I've been working on the other side of the world, her dog was like family to her." He rubbed the back of his neck. "She was in the hospital for a couple weeks for smoke inhalation and burns."

Bill winced and glanced at the scar on his right hand. He'd burned it on a camping trip last summer. The throbbing pain from that small injury had ruined the weekend for him. "Were her burns bad?"

"She didn't show me, but I saw a scar on her neck when she hugged me. But that's not all she's dealing with. The smoke hurt her lungs and voice, so she's out of a job."

"What does she do?" Bill poured the egg mixture in the pan and tossed in some grated cheese.

"She was an actress at a dinner theater in Portland."

Bill groaned inwardly. He should have known she would be an actress just like his former girlfriend. Of course, Kelsey was a drama teacher at a small college in Boston, but what was the difference? Both women liked to be on stage. No doubt Jennifer was just as attached to the big city and bright lights as Kelsey.

"They do Broadway musicals," Wes continued. "The supporting cast members serve tables and then change into costume for the show. She's a great dancer, and she has a beautiful voice, but the doctor told her she shouldn't sing until her lungs and throat have time to rest and heal."

"So, she's out of work and has nowhere to go?" The muscles in Bill's shoulders tensed. It looked like he'd be adding another roommate whether he liked it or not.

"That's right." Wes grinned and slapped him on the back, seemingly unaware of Bill's discomfort.

"What are you so happy about?"

"Oh, I wouldn't wish this kind of trouble on anyone, but I've been praying for a chance to be more involved in Jenn's life for years. And now, here it is." Wes chuckled as he pulled out a chair and sat down at the table. "You know how it feels when you pray hard for something for a long time, and then God answers, and you're just so . . . surprised."

The delight on his friend's face cut a guilty swath through Bill.

Wes looked up, his expression growing serious. "But this is your house, so it's up to you."

Bill focused on stirring the eggs. How could he say no? Wes paid his share of the rent and utilities, and he split the grocery bill even though he often ate at Lauren's.

"I guess I could send her over to Lauren's if you don't want her to stay here."

Bill shook his head. "No. It's okay. She can stay. Sounds like she needs a break."

"She needs more than that. This is our chance to show her how much God loves her and how faith makes a difference in our everyday lives. We can be the Bible she hasn't read, the Jesus she's never considered."

Bill turned off the burner and looked at Wes. "Isn't that the way we're supposed to be living anyway?"

Wes grinned, his eyes bright. "Of course, but sharing with Jenn might be it a little more challenging than that."

"Go on. I'm listening." Bill scooped the eggs onto his plate and dropped two slices of bread in the toaster.

"She knows where I stand with the Lord, and what I did as a missionary, but she's pretty closed to discussions about God or faith."

"How come?"

"I'm not sure. I thought she made a commitment to the Lord when she was young at church camp, but after we lost our parents she had to live with our aunt and uncle, and she stopped going to church. Life's been hard for her, and now she has to work through all these new losses."

"Sounds like it won't be easy to reach her after all that's happened."

Wes leaned back and smiled. "You're probably right, but don't forget, 'What's impossible for man is possible for God.'"

Bill nodded. "Like I always say, you're a man of great faith." He kept his tone light, but uncomfortable questions rose in his mind. What part did Wes expect him to play in all this? His faith ran deep, but he wasn't a missionary like his friend. He was a man of action rather than words. And how could he help Jennifer see her need for God when he wasn't exactly thrilled that she'd invaded his home?

He bowed his head and thanked the Lord for his food, but he couldn't ignore the Spirit's tug on his conscience. *Lord, help me change my attitude. I know you ask me to love others as Christ loves me, and that even includes dangerously attractive females who belong back in the city on center stage.*

CHAPTER 3

Jennifer rolled over and squinted at the soft light filtering through the window. A chorus of birds sang somewhere nearby. She rubbed her hand across her eyes, trying to focus and make sense of the scene.

What time was it? She glanced at the clock on the nightstand. Ten after eight. Was it morning or evening? The fuzzy sensation in her head and the strangeness of waking up in someone else's room sent an uneasy shiver through her.

Lying back, she lifted her left hand and traced the twisted patterns of skin on her neck, shoulder and arm.

It wasn't a dream. The scars were real. The fire had swept through her apartment and burned everything. Her beloved dog, Beau, was gone, and her fiancé, Phillip, had disappeared after one look at her hideous burns.

She squeezed her eyes shut against the painful memories and let her hand fall to her side, but she couldn't banish the angry, hopeless feeling rising in her heart.

Hadn't she already been through enough—losing her parents and then living with relatives who barely put up with her until she turned eighteen and their legal responsibility ended?

Downstairs, a door closed. Footsteps crunched across the stone path. Two doors slammed, and a motor rumbled to life.

Jennifer eased herself into a sitting position, careful not to use her right arm. She crossed to the bedroom window and peeked out in time to see the black truck backing out of the driveway. Bill sat behind the wheel, and her brother filled the passenger seat. A small blue Toyota sat on the far side of the driveway.

So, the truck belonged to Bill. The Toyota must be her brother's.

She released a heavy sigh as she watched the truck disappear around the bend in the road. Then she shifted her gaze to the yard below. Dew sparkled on the grass like little prisms of shimmering light. White daisies and small purple wildflowers swayed in the breeze. She pushed open the window. Cool fresh air greeted her. It must be Tuesday morning rather than Monday evening.

Why had Wes left without checking on her or saying goodbye? She needed to talk to him and begin making plans. Uneasiness tightened her empty stomach. She pulled the window closed and wrapped her arms around herself, trying to halt another shiver.

What would she do all day by herself?

Then another question rose and tore away the tiny shred of peace she tried so hard to hold on to.

Would Wes and Bill let her stay? Where would she go if they didn't?

She closed her eyes, yearning to talk to someone who cared. If only she believed there was a God who listened and answered prayer. But she'd given up that fantasy the night she'd sat in the emergency room and prayed her parents would live.

The answer to her plea had been a devastating "no." So she'd closed her heart and never whispered a prayer since.

SURRENDERED HEARTS

∽

BILL TAPPED his pen on his desk and tried to focus on the grant application in front of him. He just needed to double-check the changes he'd made to be sure there were no more typos. He shifted in the chair and glanced at his watch. Ten thirty-seven.

Why hadn't Jennifer called?

He tossed the pen aside and rose from behind his desk. Leaving his office, he strode into the Nature Center auditorium looking for Wes. He found him up on a ladder hanging a new sign for the reptile exhibit. "Do you know what time it is?"

Wes checked his watch. "About ten-forty."

Bill huffed. "Well, aren't you going to do anything about it?"

"What do you mean?" Wes climbed down the ladder.

"I mean, don't you think it's a little strange that your sister is still sleeping after nineteen hours?"

A small smile twitched at the corners of Wes's mouth. "Are you worried she's turned into Sleeping Beauty or something?"

Bill scowled. "No, it's just not normal for someone to sleep that long. What if something's wrong because of her burns or the smoke inhalation? Don't you think you should check on her?"

Wes rubbed his chin. "I could call, but if she's still asleep, she probably needs the rest. When she wakes up, she'll find that note we left on the kitchen table."

"If she wakes up," Bill grumbled under his breath. "So, you're just going to wait?"

"I thought I'd go home at lunch and check on her if she hasn't called by noon."

Bill looked at his watch again. "Okay, why don't you go ahead and take an early lunch? I don't mind keeping an eye . .

." His words faded as Jennifer stepped through the front door.

Her hesitant glance swept the room, stalling when she spotted Bill. Emotion flickered in her eyes. She touched the collar and top button of her pale green blouse then smoothed her hand down the sleeve.

"Hey, Jenn." Wes crossed the room and greeted his sister with a hug. "You look rested." He smiled as he surveyed her, affection in his eyes.

She laughed softly. "I slept a little longer than I expected." Her gaze met Bill's and held. "Hello, Bill."

"Morning." He nodded and crossed his arms, but that did little to shield him from the way her arrival stirred his senses.

Her cheeks flushed pink, and she shifted her focus to her brother. "I saw your note, so I decided to come see you. I hope it's okay I used your car."

"That's why I left you the keys. Use it whenever you like."

"Thanks." She glanced around the auditorium at the display cases lining the walls.

Bill couldn't help noticing the way her honey-blond hair fell in shiny waves over her shoulders. Today her eyes looked soft green shaded by long dark lashes. He frowned and shifted his gaze away.

Jennifer turned to Wes. "Do you have time to show me around?"

"Sure, I'd love to give you a tour."

She smiled and nodded, admiration for her brother shining in her eyes.

What would it feel like to have Jennifer look at him that way? The question rattled Bill, and he quickly shook it off.

"Let's start in the office. I want to show you Bill's bird collection."

Bill lifted his hand. "I'm sure Jennifer's not interested in seeing a bunch of stuffed birds."

"Oh, I'd love to see them, if it's all right with you." She sent him a hesitant smile, waiting for his response.

A slow warming started in his chest, moved up his neck, and flushed his face and ears. Did she realize the power of her smile? He quickly glanced away, silently mocking himself for being such a fool. She was an actress. She knew exactly what she was doing.

"Sure. Go ahead." Bill's tone betrayed his irritation. He didn't believe she was truly interested in his birds. It was more likely that she wanted to humor him or impress her brother.

Wes led the way, telling Jennifer about the Nature Center programs and special events they planned for the community and tourists who visited the area.

Bill followed them into the office. They seemed to understand each other with just a glance or a few words. He decided it must be a brother-sister connection he knew nothing about, and it left him feeling like an outsider.

Jennifer gazed at the case holding his bird collection. Her lips parted, and her eyes widened. She ran her hand down the side glass panel as though she wished she could touch the birds. "This is amazing. Where did you find all of them?"

Bill hesitated for a moment. "My grandfather and dad started the collection about thirty years ago. They passed it on to me, and I've added a few more birds since then."

She leaned closer. "What's the name of that little blue one with the orange chest?"

"That's an Eastern Bluebird. My dad found him in Maine."

"He's beautiful," she whispered, awe filling her voice. She turned and looked at him, a new interest in her eyes.

Conflicting emotions battled in Bill's spirit. He turned away and pointed to the stuffed raccoon on his filing cabinet. "I have a few mammals too."

"Mammals? How did you get all these?" She frowned

slightly and narrowed her eyes. "You didn't kill them, did you?"

"No, all the animals on display here died from natural causes or accidents." He stepped over to the filing cabinet and ran his hand over the raccoon's back, admiring the soft fur and unique coloring. "This little ring tail is one of my favorites."

She crossed her arms and lifted her gaze to the stuffed moose head mounted over his desk. "What about that one? I'm sure he died of natural causes, too." Sarcasm tinged her voice.

Bill straightened. "I'm not sure. I inherited him when I took over the job as head naturalist."

"Killing animals for recreation is cruel. I don't believe in hunting." She lifted her eyebrows and focused on him, waiting for a response.

Bill wasn't a hunter, but her attitude hit a nerve. "Hunting big game is a valid method of wildlife management. Seasons are set based on the maximum population a particular habitat can sustain. Hunting actually protects the environment if it's done the right way for the right reasons."

Jennifer's cheeks flushed pink. "It's never right to kill an animal so you can hang his head on your wall."

Wes chuckled and patted his sister's shoulder. "Jenn, I promise you Bill and I did not shoot any of the animals we have on display. It's our job to teach people to respect the environment and take care of wildlife. We're always on the lookout for injured animals, and if we find any, we take them to the wildlife rehab center."

She seemed to relax a little, but she still studied Bill as though she wasn't quite certain her brother's words were true.

Bill returned her gaze with a challenge of his own. Memories of Kelsey's disdain for his job flooded his mind. She'd begged him to quit and look for a teaching position in Boston.

If he settled in the city, they could continue their relationship. She didn't care about his goals and desires. Only her dreams were important.

The memories faded, but they left him feeling hollow and disappointed. He glanced at Jennifer again. Maybe she was an animal lover, but it was clear she didn't respect him or appreciate his work as a naturalist.

That was fine with him. It gave him one more good reason to stay far away from Jennifer Evans.

CHAPTER 4

*J*enn set her coffee cup on the counter by the sink and glanced out the open kitchen window at the quiet meadow surrounding Bill and Wes's house. Late afternoon sunlight filtered through the tall trees beyond the yard. A large bumblebee buzzed past the screen. A bird called from the branch of a nearby pine tree.

That was all she heard. No cars or trucks barreling past. No blaring sirens or city sounds to interrupt the peaceful moment.

Bill's den door opened, pulling her attention away from the window. She turned and watched him step out.

He wore a dark-green shirt and khaki slacks. She couldn't help noticing how handsome he looked. Pressing her lips together, she turned away.

He grabbed his keys off the end of the counter. "Ready to go?"

She nodded and picked up her purse from the kitchen table. The three of them were headed to Lauren's for dinner. What would it be like to meet Wes's fiancée? Biting her lower lip, she checked the button on the cuff of her long-sleeve shirt and tried to push away the uncomfortable thought of having to explain the explosion and fire again. Her stomach tightened just thinking about it.

Bill glanced at his watch and then toward the stairs. "Hey, Wes, you ready?"

"I'll be right down."

Bill crossed to the front door and turned back to look at her. "Come on. I'll drive."

With an uneasy glance over her shoulder, she followed Bill outside. They'd hardly spoken since he'd returned from the Nature Center an hour ago. He obviously hadn't liked the way she'd questioned him that morning about the animals on display.

He opened the truck's passenger door for her and waited for her to climb into the hot cab. Then he walked around and got in his side. As soon as he started the engine, he pushed the button to roll down both windows and flipped the air conditioner on high, never saying a word.

Jenn fiddled with the handle of her purse and watched the house, waiting for her brother.

The front door opened. Wes hustled down the steps and approached the truck. "Think I'll drive over." He grinned at them. "Maybe I can talk Lauren into letting me stay a little later."

Jenn nodded and reached for the door handle.

Wes lifted his hand and took a step back. "Why don't you ride with Bill? It'll give you two a chance to talk." He smiled at her and headed over to his own car.

Bill drummed his fingers on the steering wheel. "Are you okay with that?"

"Sure." She stared out the front window. Being stuck in this hot truck with a man who obviously didn't like her was not her idea of a good time, but what choice did she have?

Bill backed out of the driveway and headed south on Shelton Road, his eyes focused straight ahead and his mouth set in a determined line.

What was he thinking? Probably silently repeating every critical remark she'd made at the nature center.

After two minutes of awkward silence, she glanced over at him. "I'm sorry for what I said about the stuffed animals."

He didn't answer, but she saw the muscle in his jaw twitch.

"It's just that hunting seems heartless to me."

His blue-gray eyes narrowed. "Yeah, I got that."

When he didn't say any more, she released an irritated huff. What was his problem? She'd made the first move and apologized. Why couldn't he at least be civil? She crossed her arms and stared out the window again. Fine. If he didn't want to talk, she could be quiet.

A minute or so later, Bill cleared his throat. "Wes told me you've always liked animals." His gentle tone surprised her.

She glanced at him, trying to guess what had spurred his attitude shift. "I've had a lot of pets."

"Such as?"

A smile tugged at her lips. She couldn't help it. She loved to talk about her animals. "Fish, of course, and I had a turtle. He got so big we had to let him go in the river. Then I had a frog, four mice, two rats, five rabbits, three parakeets, a batch of baby chicks, and two dogs."

He lifted his brows. "All at the same time?"

She laughed. "No. Over the years, a few at a time."

"So, which one was your favorite?"

"My dog Beau." Her throat tightened, and she could barely speak. "He was a beautiful golden retriever."

"And what was so special about him?"

"He always greeted me at the door when I came home, wagging his tail and looking up at me like I was his favorite person in all the world."

"Sounds like a nice dog."

"He was more than that." She swallowed, hoping she could make her voice sound normal. "When I was fifteen my parents were killed in a car accident." She waited for his reaction, but his calm, steady expression didn't change. "I guess you knew that. You were Wes's roommate then, right?"

He nodded. "It was hard on Wes. But it must have been really rough for you."

"I made it through." She steeled her heart against those painful memories.

"No, really. It must have been hard losing both your parents when you were so young."

She stiffened, not wanting to remember the pain or go there with him. "I learned to deal with it. I lived with my aunt and uncle, and as soon as I was eighteen, I left and lived on my own. That's when I got Beau."

Bill nodded slowly. "So, losing him must bring up a lot of painful memories for you."

Hot tears pricked her eyes, and she looked away. Why did everyone want to play psychiatrist and force her to relive all the pain? What was the point? She had to be strong and focus on the future. That was the only way she'd made it through these last few years.

Bill flipped on his blinker and turned into a long gravel drive. Large maple trees lined both sides creating a thick, green canopy overhead. "This is Long Meadow." He nodded toward the house and then pointed to a barn on the right. "That's Lauren's art and antique gallery. She just opened last March, about the same time she and Wes got engaged."

Jenn studied the large red barn surrounded by well-maintained flowerbeds and a lush green lawn. The gravel drive widened to provide a parking area between the barn and house.

Bill pulled in, and she turned her attention to the large, two-story farmhouse painted light yellow with white shutters. It had an inviting wrap-around porch and a shady front yard where a child's rope swing hung from the branch of an old maple tree. Flowerbeds with bright annuals and rose bushes in full bloom surrounded the porch.

Wes parked his Toyota next to them, closer to the barn. As he climbed out of his car, a pretty redhead stepped out the barn door and waved. A broad smile lit up Wes's face as he met her halfway and pulled her into an embrace.

Jenn lowered her gaze, unfastened her seatbelt and bent to pick up her purse. Her passenger door opened, and Bill looked in at her.

Heat flooded her cheeks. She hadn't been waiting for him to open her door. She'd wanted to give Wes and Lauren a moment alone before she interrupted them. She mumbled her thanks to Bill and climbed out of the truck.

Wes took Lauren's hand and walked toward them. "Jenn, I want you to meet Lauren."

Before she could respond, Lauren stepped forward and gave her a big hug. "I'm so glad you're here. This makes everything perfect."

"Thanks." Pain shot through Jenn's right shoulder as Lauren squeezed tighter. She closed her eyes and gritted her teeth. When Lauren finally let go, Jenn stepped back, her shoulder and arm throbbing.

"Come on. Let's go inside. Aunt Tilley has dinner ready." Lauren took Wes's hand and they walked toward the house.

Bill followed with one brief glance over his shoulder in Jenn's direction.

Jenn climbed the back steps and slowed to look around the porch. Two round-back wicker chairs with yellow and blue striped cushions sat near the back door with a small wicker table between them. Four pots of bright red geraniums hung from hooks under the edge of the porch roof. This looked like a great spot to relax and read a book. Jenn smiled at that thought. What a different life Lauren must lead from what Jenn was used to.

Back in Portland, her days consisted of sleeping in late,

meeting her fellow actors at the dinner theater around one, and practicing musical numbers all afternoon until it was time to grab a quick dinner and dress for the evening show.

"Everything okay?" Bill stood in the doorway, waiting for her. Concern and a hint of some other emotion flickered in his eyes.

She nodded and forced a small smile. "Sure. Everything's fine."

But she couldn't push away the empty feeling in her heart. What would she do now that she couldn't walk out on the stage and hear the applause after each song? How would she fill her days?

CHAPTER 5

Bill settled back in his chair, took a sip of his coffee, and glanced around the table. Dinner with Lauren and Tilley was always a treat, and tonight was no exception. The great food, friendly conversation and comfortable atmosphere made him feel like part of the family.

Tilley had outdone herself preparing a chicken and rice casserole covered in a cheesy sauce that melted in his mouth. Of course, the homemade rolls, fresh spinach salad, and tender asparagus weren't bad either. No one cooked like Tilley Woodman.

Tilley bustled into the dining room bringing a stack of dessert dishes and extra forks. Lauren followed, carrying a delicious-looking strawberry pie and a bowl of whipped cream.

"I hope you all saved room for dessert." Tilley set the plates on the dining room table.

Wes moaned. "You should've warned me." He scooted his chair back and stretched. "But I think I can handle it." He turned to Lauren's son, Toby. "How about you, buddy? You ready for some pie?"

Toby grinned at Wes with glowing eyes. "I love pie." The

little boy turned and watched his great aunt slice the brightly glazed dessert.

Bill could hardly believe the changes he'd seen in Toby over the last few months. Though he still struggled in his first grade class because of his learning disabilities, the school year was almost over, and he was looking forward to summer vacation. He seemed more settled and content now. With Lauren's constant love and Wes's involvement, he was learning how to cope and seemed to finally be enjoying the happy childhood he deserved.

"Can I cut you a piece of pie, Bill?"

"Sounds great. Thanks, Tilley."

Lauren's aunt halted mid-slice and looked up. "I'm sorry, Jennifer. Where are my manners? You're our special guest tonight. I should've asked you first. Would you like a piece, dear?"

Jennifer looked uncomfortable at being singled out, but she smiled and nodded. "Sure, thanks. Just a small piece."

Bill glanced across the table and studied Wes's sister. She'd been awfully quiet during dinner, only answering questions that were directed to her. His mind drifted back to their conversation on the ride over. He'd been surprised by her apology. It left him with a nagging feeling that he'd misjudged her. Her love for her pets and interest in animals seemed genuine. Maybe she was an actress, but that didn't mean everything she did was an act. Those tears in her eyes when she talked about losing her dog had to be real.

Bill frowned and scooped up his first bite of pie, savoring the sweet berries and cool whipped cream.

He needed to stop worrying about Jennifer Evans. She was not his concern. Wes and Lauren would take care of her.

But when he looked up, his gaze connected with Jenn's. For a brief moment he caught a glimpse past the wall she seemed to have put up to keep everyone at a distance. Behind it he saw a frightened young woman with a wounded heart.

He blinked, breaking the connection. Gripping his coffee cup, he took a big gulp and tried to shake off the painful impression.

"I took a drive over to West Harmon today and stopped at that shop Julia told me about." Lauren smiled at Wes. "I think I found the perfect bridesmaid's dress."

Wes lifted his eyebrows and smiled. "Great."

Tilley sat down. "What's it like, dear?"

"Floor-length, kind of A-line with a natural waist. I didn't think I wanted a strapless dress, but this has an organza jacket over the top with three-quarter length sleeves. I've got a picture of it in my purse." Lauren left the table and returned a few seconds later. She handed the picture to Tilley.

Her aunt held it out at arm's length and squinted. "Oh, it's pretty. I like the beads on the bodice." Tilley passed the picture to Wes.

He took a quick look. "Looks nice, but I thought you wanted blue dresses." He passed it to Bill.

Bill glanced at the dress. It looked good to him, but he didn't know an A-line from a B-line, so he wasn't sure his opinion mattered. He handed the picture across the table to Jennifer.

"The owner said she could order it in periwinkle blue for us. She showed me a fabric sample. It looks perfect." She smiled at Jennifer. "Maybe you could come with me and see how you like it."

Jennifer's gaze darted from the picture to Lauren. "I guess I could."

Lauren smiled, her eyes shining. "Well, I hope so, because I want to be sure the dress works for you."

Jenn stared at her. "You want me to be in the wedding?"

"Yes!" Lauren laughed. "I'm sorry. I guess that wasn't a very nice way to ask you." She set her fork down. "Wes and I would like you to be my bridesmaid. We don't have a very big wedding party. My friend, Julia Berkley, is my maid of honor, and Bill is Wes's best man. Of course, Toby will be up there with us, too."

The color drained from Jenn's face. Her hand trembled as she laid her cloth napkin on the table. "Well, I . . . excuse me." She pushed back her chair and fled to the kitchen.

Lauren turned to Wes. "I guess I shouldn't have put her on the spot like that."

"Don't worry. She'll be okay. She's probably just worried about the cost of the dress or something." Wes stared toward the kitchen doorway, a perplexed look on his face.

Bill stood and snatched the empty pitcher off the table. "Think I'll get us some more water."

Wes and Lauren's whispered words of concern faded as Bill walked into kitchen. A quick glance around the room told him Jennifer must have escaped to the small bathroom off the kitchen. He refilled the pitcher, then took an ice tray from the freezer and slowly dropped the cubes into the water one at a time.

The bathroom door opened. Jennifer stepped out.

"Everything okay?" he asked.

"Yes, thanks." Her smile looked forced, and her red eyes and splotchy cheeks told him she'd been crying.

"What happened out there?" He nodded toward the dining room.

"Nothing." She wrapped her arms around herself, but she didn't walk away. "I guess I'm just . . . feeling a little emotional."

He set the ice cube tray on the counter. "How come? You don't want to be in the wedding?"

"No, that's not it. It's just. . ." She glanced at the ceiling and bit her trembling lower lip. "I don't understand why Lauren would ask me to be her bridesmaid. I don't even know her, and I feel like I hardly know Wes."

She slowly shook her head. "I only wrote him a few times while he was working in the Middle East. I didn't email him very often either, even though that would have been the easiest thing in the world." She pressed her lips together. "Then after he was arrested, it was too late."

"You had no way of knowing that would happen. None of us did."

"I tried to help him. I contacted some congressmen and wrote a few letters to government officials, but after a while I ran out of ideas and hope." She brushed a tear off her cheek. "But I'm the only family he has. I shouldn't have given up. If I'd kept at it, he wouldn't have been stuck in that awful prison for eighteen months." Shuddering, she rubbed her hands down her arms.

He wished he could give her a comforting hug, but he didn't know if she would appreciate that. "Don't be so hard on yourself. That was a tough situation. There wasn't much anyone could do except pray."

"I suppose." She released a shaky sigh. "But I still can't imagine why they want me in their wedding."

"You're his sister. He loves you. And I guess he figures he's only getting married once, so you better be there to see it happen." He grinned, hoping he could tease her out of her sadness. "Come, on. It'll be fun. Wes and I are going to wear these stiff-as-a-board penguin suits. We'll have to pose for a thousand photos and smile until we feel like our faces are going to crack and fall off.

"Sounds wonderful," She muttered and reached for a tissue from the box on the counter, but a small smile lifted the corners of her mouth.

That spurred him on. "Oh, it will be. I promise. And I don't want to be the only one who's suffering. So, you have to get all dressed up and wear tight, new shoes that'll pinch your feet and make you want to cry." He paused realizing he was probably getting carried away. "Seriously, they both want you in the wedding."

She glanced up at him. "I suppose you're right, but what

do I say now? I feel so stupid. They probably think I don't like Lauren or the dress or . . ."

"Just tell them the truth."

She released a choked laugh. "What? That I'm totally selfish, and I don't deserve half the kindness they've shown me?"

"No. Say thanks, I'd love to be in your wedding."

"Just like that?"

"Yep. Just like that."

"All right, but . . ." She bit her lip and looked at him hesitantly.

"What?"

"The dress . . . I don't think—"

"What? You'd look great in that dress." As soon as the words left his mouth, he felt his neck and ears burn. "I mean, it's a great dress, but if you don't like it—"

"No. I like it. I just don't think it's . . . right for me."

"Then go with Lauren and pick out another one. You heard her. She wants your opinion." Jennifer still looked doubtful, so he added, "Lauren's sweet. I'm sure she'll listen to whatever you say. Give her a chance."

She smiled, and her gaze settled on him. "Okay. Thanks."

"For?"

"Listening and talking me out of this weird emotional . . . thing."

He chuckled. "Not a problem."

But as he followed Jenn into the dining room doubts circled through his mind. Had he'd made a mistake stepping in like that? Wasn't Wes the one who wanted to get closer to her? He cast that thought aside. Wes wouldn't mind. He'd be grateful.

But he sensed a warning in his spirit. He needed to be careful and not invest too much in this friendship. When the wedding was over, Jenn would be headed home to Oregon.

Bill flipped the page, read the final lines of the chapter, and groaned to himself. How could he stop there? He checked the clock on his bedroom end table and found it was after eleven. If he didn't hit the sack soon, he'd pay for it tomorrow.

Sleeping in was not an option. He was scheduled to lead a large homeschool group on a stream stomp and frog and salamander hunt at 9:00 am. Oh joy. He chuckled to himself, knowing he wouldn't trade his job for any other.

He set the novel on his nightstand then stood and stretched. Pushing aside his bedroom curtain, he checked the driveway out front. A full moon hung just above the treetops, spreading silver light over the yard and driveway.

No sign of Wes or his Toyota. He probably had more wedding plans to discuss with Lauren, or maybe they were just enjoying some quiet moments in front of the fire. Must be nice. Bill huffed and tossed that mental picture aside.

As he walked out of his room, he glanced across the hall at the closed bedroom door. He'd heard Jennifer's soft footsteps on the stairs over an hour ago. She was probably sound asleep in there by now. He shook off thoughts of her and headed for the bathroom. After he'd brushed his teeth, he looked for the glass that usually sat on the counter, but it wasn't there.

Then it hit him. The bathroom looked cleaner than the last time he'd used it. There wasn't a splash on the mirror or a smudge on the counter or sink. He scanned the room. Fresh towels hung on the bar by the shower, and the corner wastebasket was empty instead of overflowing.

Jennifer must have cleaned up, because it sure hadn't been him or Wes. He appreciated her help, but it felt a little like an invasion of his private space.

Well, this wasn't his private space anymore.

Looking in the mirror, he grimaced, remembering how the bathroom looked earlier. No wonder she scrubbed everything spotless. Everyone knew women didn't like grungy bathrooms.

He sighed and rubbed his forehead. Why hadn't he thought of that? Well, there was nothing he could do about it now, except thank her in the morning.

Treading softly downstairs, he walked into the dark living room and reached for the light switch. A rustling movement on the couch stopped him. He crept across the room and peeked over the back of the couch.

Moonlight flowed through the sliding glass door, illuminating a petite form curled up under a light blanket.

Surprise rippled through him. What was Jennifer doing sleeping down here? He stepped back, hoping she hadn't heard him and stole into the kitchen.

The small light over the stove had been left on. He noticed the clear counters and empty dish drainer. When had she cleaned the kitchen? Probably after they returned from Lauren's and before she cleaned the bathroom. But he wasn't certain because he'd retreated to his room to read as soon as they came home.

He shook his head recalling the stack of dirty dishes he'd left in the sink. Now he owed her a double thank you.

As he reached in the cabinet for a glass, he saw a note on the counter. Lifting the paper toward the light, he read the message.

Wes,

I'm sleeping downstairs on the couch tonight. I don't want you to give up your bed for me anymore. You need your sleep so you can get up early and go to work. Besides, you're too tall for the couch, but it's not a problem for me. I know you won't like it, but please let me do this one small thing for you.

Thanks for asking me to be in your wedding. I'm honored you want me to share that special day with you and Lauren. I'm sorry I was so weird about it when Lauren asked me tonight. (The next few words were scribbled out.) I'll explain sometime. I really do want to be there for you on your wedding day. I love you, Wes. Thanks for letting me stay here. That means a lot to me.

Love,

Jenn

Warmth flooded his chest as he read the last few sentences again. Letting Jennifer stay was the right decision. Her heart already seemed to be softening toward her brother, and hopefully that would lead her one step closer to renewing her relationship with the Lord.

He scooted the note over under the light so Wes would be sure to see it. He grabbed a clean glass from the cabinet and headed back through the living room.

As he passed the couch, he stopped and looked down at Jennifer once more. Silvery moonlight highlighted the contours of her softly rounded cheeks and straight nose. He stepped closer, watching the slight movement of her eyelids. He smiled. She must be dreaming. His gaze moved to her slightly parted lips.

He swallowed and closed his eyes. What was he doing?

Jennifer sighed and shifted to another position.

His eyes flew open. He froze, his heart banging in his chest.

She'd rolled to her side, and her long hair fanned out over the pillow, exposing a trail of twisted skin that started at the hairline behind her right ear and extended to her collarbone where it disappeared into the neck of her t-shirt.

He clenched his teeth and made himself study the scars, hoping familiarity would ease his gut-wrenching reaction. That burn had to have hurt more than anything he had ever experienced. How far did it go? He immediately squelched that thought. But as he remembered the clothes she'd worn over the last few days, he realized they all had long sleeves and collars even though the weather had been warm.

A new realization washed over him. Those scars had cost her more than physical pain and the loss of her home and dog. Jenn was a beautiful young woman, an actress whose career required a flawless appearance. What would she do now? And what about her heart and spirit? Had her burns made her believe that God didn't care and wasn't watching out for her?

A sorrowful heaviness draped over his shoulders. He blew out a deep breath, yearning to do something to right this wrong.

Father, please heal Jenn's scars, those you showed me tonight and those in her heart. Use the pain and loss she's been through to bring her closer to You. Thanks for letting me see so I can understand a little more of what she is dealing with. Show me how to help her. "Amen," he whispered.

Then he gently pulled up the blanket and tucked it around her shoulders. For a split second he thought about bending down to kiss her cheek, but he turned away and headed upstairs.

CHAPTER 6

*J*enn carefully lifted the lid of the waffle iron and poured in a cup of creamy white batter. It bubbled and sizzled as it spread over the hot griddle. Satisfied she'd added enough, she lowered the lid and watched the steam escape around the edges.

Breakfast was her favorite meal, and cooking for others made it even better. Hopefully, Wes and Bill wouldn't mind her getting up early to make waffles.

The sound of footsteps overhead made her stomach tighten. She wiped her hands on a kitchen towel and checked the table. Everything was ready. She'd put on the coffee, made the orange juice, sliced the strawberries, warmed the maple syrup, and set three places. In the center of the table, she'd placed a small jar filled with wildflowers she'd picked in the yard. Their cheerful little faces seemed to smile up at her, giving her courage a boost.

She definitely needed that this morning. It was time she and Wes talked about a plan for the summer. She couldn't just sponge off him and his roommate indefinitely.

Footsteps descend the stairs and crossed the living room. She looked up as Bill walked into the kitchen wearing jeans and a navy knit shirt with the Wild River Resort logo embroidered over the pocket.

"Good morning." She sent him a bright smile. But her stomach quivered as she noticed the healthy glow of his clean-shaven face. His dark wavy hair, still damp from his shower, curled behind his ears and touched his collar at the back.

"Morning." He frowned slightly as he studied the table. "What's going on?"

She stared at him, her courage fading. "I . . . I'm making waffles."

He lifted his dark eyebrows and shot her a curious glance. "You didn't have to do that."

She turned toward the sink. "I know, but I wanted to do something . . ." Her mind spun, searching for an explanation. What could she say? That she couldn't face sitting around all day feeling useless? That she had to prove she wasn't a burden? That she'd cleaned and cooked and slept on an uncomfortable couch so they'd consider her helpful and wouldn't send her away?

Bill stepped up behind her. "I'm sorry. That didn't come out right. Waffles sound great."

Waffles! She spun toward the counter. The red light on top of the waffle iron had come on. "Oh, shoot!" She jerked the lid up and grabbed a fork. A dark-brown waffle stuck to the upper griddle. Her hand slipped as she tried jabbed it with a fork. Scorching pain shot through her fingertips. She gasped and jerked back, dropping the fork on the counter.

Bill grabbed her elbow and steered her toward the sink. Before she could ask what he was doing, he turned on the cold water and thrust her fingers under the icy, gushing stream.

Hovering behind her, he held her arm steady. "Just keep your hand in the water."

She looked over her shoulder at him, but then quickly

glanced away as tears gathered in her eyes. Her fingers stung, but that wasn't what made her cry. Self-doubt programmed into her from years of criticism rose to the surface. Why hadn't she been more careful? How could she forget the danger of a hot appliance or the pain burns could cause? Couldn't she do anything right?

Bill eased his hold on her arm and stepped back. "I'll unplug that waffle iron."

"Wait, I still have a lot of batter." She pulled her hand out of the water and turned it over. Pain throbbed from the pink, oval-shaped welts marking the tips of her index and middle finger.

Bill returned to her side. "Hey, it's not time to take your fingers out yet." Concern filled his eyes as he gently guided her hand back under the stream of cool water. "This'll help reduce the pain and any possible swelling. But you've got to give it a little more time."

She nodded, grateful for his kindness and the soothing tone of his voice. "I'm okay. It's not a bad burn."

"Good. You stay there, and I'll take care of that crispy critter." He grinned and cocked his head toward the open waffle maker.

"I can't believe I burned it." She bit her lip. He probably thought she was a brainless blond with no cooking experience.

"Don't worry. It's not a big deal." He chuckled. "I usually burn one or two of them every time."

"Really?" Surprise filled her voice.

He nodded, picked up the fork and turned his attention to removing the scorched waffle.

She hadn't met many men who were willing to admit their mistakes. Her former fiancé never liked to say he was wrong. Appearances and putting on a good front mattered more to him.

The last time she'd seen Phillip flashed into her mind.

He'd come to the hospital the evening of the explosion and fire, and though he was an experienced actor, he hadn't been able to hide his shocked response to her burns. When he walked away, he'd taken a piece of her heart, and almost convinced her it wasn't worth fighting to recover.

He may have been wrong to desert her, but he was right about one thing. Her scars were beyond ugly, and she'd never be rid of them.

She glanced at her right arm and slowly ran her hand down her sleeve feeling the uneven texture of her skin under the thin cotton material.

Bill tossed the burnt waffle in the trash then poured in the next round of batter. "My problem is I can't wait to eat, so I sit down and start enjoying breakfast, and I forget I'm still making more waffles."

She leaned on the edge of the sink, watching his confident, easy movements. He obviously knew his way around the kitchen.

Grabbing a sponge, he wiped a few batter drips off the counter. Then he took a small plate from the cabinet and set it under the drippy measuring cup to avoid making any more mess. With a final glance at the steaming waffle iron, he walked back toward her.

"Let's see how it's doing."

She pulled her hand out of the water and held it out to him.

He turned it over and gently cradled her cold, wet fingers in his warm hand. "Looks like we got it cooled off in time. I don't think it will blister."

She swallowed, suddenly aware of his nearness and touch. He smelled clean and fresh, like herbal soap and crisp mountain air. Energy seemed to radiate from his hand and vibrate through her. She looked up. Their gazes connected and held, sending a tremor through her.

"Hey, what's going on?" Wes crossed the kitchen toward them.

"I just burned my fingers a little."

"Let's see." Wes stepped over closer, and Bill released her hand to her brother. He checked it out and looked up at Bill. "What do you think?"

"First degree. Pain should diminish in a few hours."

Wes nodded, looking relieved.

She glanced at Bill. "How do you know that?"

He sent her an easy grin. "Just an educated guess."

"Hey, tell her the truth."

"It's not important."

"Yes, it is." Wes turned to Jenn. "He's a certified wilderness first responder."

She looked back and forth between them, uncertain of what that meant.

"He's trained in CPR and first aid for just about any medical emergency we could run into at the nature center or one of our outings."

"Did you go to school for that?"

Bill nodded. "I took a course up in Maine."

Wes slapped him on the shoulder. "That training puts him right up there with an EMT." He leaned back against the kitchen counter, grinning, looking as though he enjoyed embarrassing his roommate. "He also has a BA in ecology and environmental studies and an MA in Forest Ecology."

"Stop." Bill scowled at Wes. "She doesn't care about that."

"Oh, I'm impressed." She smiled, enjoying being in the middle of their exchange. For some reason her mind shifted to Phillip again. He had pursued three different majors over six years in college but never graduated. She silently chided herself for comparing Phillip and Bill and shook off those thoughts. "I'm glad you knew what to do for this burn. Thanks."

He glanced at her hand. "How's it feeling now?"

"It just stings a little. I'll be fine. Let's eat breakfast." She turned to check the waffle iron. "Looks like the next one is done."

"Let me get it." Bill lifted the lid and used the fork to pull out a perfectly toasted waffle. "Here you go, Wes. You can do the honors."

"Man, I wish I had time. But I promised Toby I'd stop by before work." He grinned. "He has some big end-of-the-school-year project he wants to show me before he turns it in. Guess I could take that waffle with me." He snatched it from Bill's fork and took a bite. "Delicious. Thanks."

"You're welcome," Jenn called as Wes crossed the kitchen.

He grabbed his keys off the counter. "See you guys later."

She waved goodbye as he walked out the door. So much for having a talk. It looked like she'd just have to make her own plans. And first on the list was finding a job, though she wasn't sure what she was qualified to do besides acting. Even if she did find someone who would hire her, how would she get to work without a car? She'd sold hers to help cover her medical bills and living expenses for the last two months.

Bill poured more batter into the waffle iron, then looked up. "Don't worry. These look great. I'll eat all Wes's waffles and mine too."

Jenn smiled. "Okay, but save me one."

"You'll have to fight me for it." He grinned and lowered the lid on the waffle maker. "Hey, I've got to work this morning, but I'm off this afternoon. I thought I'd head into town around twelve-thirty. Want to come along?"

Jenn studied him for a moment, surprised by his invitation. A trip into town sounded better than spending the rest of the day here alone, and she might see a help wanted sign or places she could apply. "Sure, thanks."

"Great. I'll show you all the hot spots in Tipton in about two minutes."

His humor nudged her spirits a little higher, but her questions soon returned and stirred her anxious thoughts to the surface. How long would it be before Bill got tired of having her around? What would she do then?

CHAPTER 7

The bell over the door of the Tipton General Store and Post Office rang out a cheerful greeting as Jenn stepped inside. Bill followed her, closing the door behind him and setting off the bell again.

As she lifted her sunglasses and waited for her eyes to adjust to the dim light, she noticed the faint scents of peppermint, pipe smoke and fresh cut wood.

"Well, hello, stranger. I haven't seen you for a while." A man with a full, silvery beard and twinkling blue eyes greeted Bill from behind the store's wide, wooden counter. He wore a faded, green plaid shirt and peered at them through wire-rimmed glasses.

"Afternoon, Howard. How you doing?"

"I'm right as rain, and hoping it'll stay sunny."

As the men shook hands, Jenn glanced around the store and felt as though she had stepped back in time. The walls were covered with shelves filled with every kind of grocery and household item you could imagine. Glass jars holding various colored peppermint sticks stood in a neat row next to the old-fashioned cash register. Baskets of lemons, apples, potatoes, and onions sat on the floor in front of the counter.

Nearby, bundles of kindling were stacked next to boxes of fishing tackle.

Howard stroked his beard and peered at her with interest. "Who is this pretty lady?"

"This is Jennifer Evans, Wes's sister." Bill turned to her and smiled. "Jenn, this is Howard Clarkson, Tipton's postmaster, owner of this fine store, and the best horseshoe player in all Addison County."

Howard chuckled. "Thanks, but I don't know if I'll be holding on to that title much longer. Ralph McHenry's been practicing all year. Says he's gonna' show me a thing or two at the Fourth of July picnic."

Bill shook his head. "Don't worry. He'll never beat you."

"Hope you're right, or I'll be eating a lot of crow instead of my wife's fine potato salad." He chuckled and clapped his hands together. "Now then, what can I do for you two today?" Before they could answer, he stooped behind the counter and brought up a small white carton that looked like the takeout containers Jenn brought home from her favorite Chinese restaurant in Portland.

"Are you headed out fishing?" Howard slid the carton across the counter toward them. "Elmer Foster brought in some mighty fine worms just this morning. Most of 'em over six inches." He held up his hands to demonstrate the length.

Jenn shivered and took a step back, bumping into Bill.

His strong hands steadied her for a moment before he let go. "No thanks. We're just here to do a little shopping and pick up the mail. Have you sorted it yet?"

Howard snorted, looking offended. "Course I have. It's always in the boxes by ten. You know that."

Bill grinned. "Okay. Just checkin'."

Howard moseyed around the end of the counter and crossed to the opposite side of the store where he slipped through a doorway. Two seconds later he appeared behind the window set into the wall. Rows of glass-front mailboxes filled the wall nearby.

Bill leaned toward her. "Looks like the post office is now open. Come on."

Jenn stifled a giggle and followed Bill down the aisle filled with cake mixes, bags of flour and sugar, and small jars of spices. The scent of cinnamon and nutmeg tickled her nose as she walked past.

Howard rested his arms on the post office counter and leaned forward. "Can I help you?"

"I'm just checking my box." Bill turned to Jenn. "Do you need stamps or anything?"

"No thanks." But she realized there was something else she did need. Straightening her shoulders, she smiled at Howard. "Overseeing both the store and the post office must keep you pretty busy. Are you looking for any help?"

Howard frowned and brushed his hand across the counter. "Well, my wife Arlene works with me most days, but she's off visitin' her sister in Burlington right now. Betty took a spill last week and broke her wrist."

"I'm sorry." Jenn remembered the lonely days she'd spent in the hospital. It amazed her how many of her so-called friends had been too busy to visit. Or had they been frightened away by Phillip's description of her burns? "It's a good thing she has her sister nearby to help," she said softly.

"Yes, yes, it is." He stroked his beard, regarding her more closely. "But to answer your question, Tipton's a small town. And I can generally handle both the post office and store myself though Arlene's here most afternoons."

Jenn nodded, forced a small smile and tried to shake off her disappointment. She shouldn't expect to find a job the first time she asked, but it would've been nice.

Bill took his keys from his pocket and unlocked one of the post office boxes. He pulled out a small stack of mail and thumbed through the pile.

Howard peeked over the top of his glasses. "There's a letter in there from your folks."

Bill glanced up at him. "Howard, you're supposed to sort the mail, not read it."

"It's not reading if I'm just lookin' at the return addresses."

Bill winked at Jenn, and then he pulled out the letter.

Jenn glanced at the upper left corner trying not to be too obvious. Highland, NC. She'd never heard of it, but she imagined North Carolina was a beautiful state with plenty of open space and woodlands. She could picture Bill coming from a place like that.

Bill dropped two advertisements in the trashcan then tucked a phone bill and the letter from his family in his back pocket. He glanced at her. "Okay. You have the shopping list?"

She nodded and took it out of her purse, but she couldn't help wondering why he didn't open the letter from home. She would have given anything to receive a letter from her parents. But that was impossible now. They'd been gone almost ten years. In some ways, it seemed like a long time ago, but on other days, she felt like the accident had happened last week. Either way, it definitely wasn't long enough to stop the pain that echoed through her heart each time she remembered losing them.

Fifteen minutes later they dropped off three bags of groceries in the back of Bill's truck. As they crossed the street toward the Tipton National Bank, Jenn glanced over her shoulder. "Are you sure it's okay to leave those groceries sitting out like that?"

Bill sent her a quizzical look. "Sure. Why?"

"But anyone walking by could just help themselves," she added.

"That kind of thing doesn't happen around here."

"Never?"

Bill chuckled and sent her a lazy grin. "Well, Roy Chambers says someone stole his canoe paddles out of the back of his truck, but the word around town is he tipped over when he was fishing at Mirror Lake and lost 'em there." Bill pushed open the front door of the bank and stood back for her to walk through first.

That simple gesture pleased her more that she would have imagined. "Thanks." She smiled up at him, deciding she could definitely get used to this kind of treatment.

She stood back and watched as Bill passed a check and deposit slip to the middle-aged woman behind the teller's window. They greeted each other by name, and the teller asked him about the stream stomp at the nature center. Bill launched into recounting a funny incident that had left him and several kids muddy and soaked.

How would it feel to be known and greeted like that, to live in a town where your roots went down deep, and everyone treated you like friends and family? All her life she'd lived in a large city where anonymous salespeople barely spoke to her and almost never cracked a smile. And things were not much better at her aunt and uncle's home. Stern and emotionally distant, they'd always left her feeling like an outsider.

Bill tucked the cash from the teller in his wallet and slipped it into his back pocket. "Thanks, Mary Ann. You have a good day, and tell Chuck I said hello."

"Oh, I will. And you and your friend have a nice day, too." The teller smiled at Jenn, a hint of curiosity in her brown eyes. The woman lifted her hand and waved goodbye.

Jenn stepped outside as Bill held the door open for her again. The scent of fresh baked bread drifted past. Jenn sniffed and glanced around. "Wow, do you smell that?"

Bill pulled in a deep breath. "Yeah. I bet it's coming from the Green Mountain Bakery or the Wild River Café." He nodded down the street. "Are you hungry?"

"Starved."

"Let's go then."

They walked past Mc Cullen's Pharmacy following the delicious scent. The door of Berkley Real Estate opened, and a young woman stepped out. When she spotted Bill, she smiled and waved.

"Hey, Julia." Bill returned her wave.

The name clicked, and Jenn guessed she was the friend Lauren had asked to be her maid of honor. She wore a multicolored flowered skirt and a neatly pressed, blue sleeveless blouse that revealed her flawless skin and glowing tan.

Bill and Julia exchanged a hug.

A ripple of uneasiness flowed through Jenn as she watched them. Evidently, Bill and Julia were also good friends. And no wonder—Julia was adorable. She had light-brown hair styled in a cute, short cut that showed off her dainty ears and slender neck.

Julia stepped back, adjusted the strap on her brown leather purse and shifted her focus to Jenn. Her smile dimmed slightly, and questions shimmered in her pretty blue eyes.

Bill turned to Jenn. "This is Julia Berkley. She's a real estate agent." He pointed to the office on their right. "She works here with her Dad."

Jenn extended her hand. "Hi, I'm Jennifer Evans."

Julia's smile brightened. "Lauren told me you were in town. Are you staying until the wedding?"

Jenn nodded, discomfort over her situation stealing away the explanation.

"Are you looking for a place to rent?" With only a brief pause, Julia continued, "There's a cute little two-bedroom cottage on the outskirts of town that just became available. The owners can't come up this summer, so they want me to find someone to rent it. It's a great location and totally furnished." Julia looked at her expectantly.

Jenn's mouth suddenly felt parched. "Well . . . I'm not sure. I don't—"

"Jenn's staying with us." Bill's calm, even tone settled the matter.

"Oh." Julia's gaze darted from Jenn to Bill.

Warmth flooded Jenn's cheeks, but she was grateful Bill hadn't shared the details of the explosion and fire or her empty bank account.

"Well, that'll give you more time with your brother."

Jenn nodded. "I hope so."

"Lauren said you're going to be in the wedding with us. Did you see the dress she picked out? It should look pretty in periwinkle blue." Julia turned her 100-watt smile on Bill. "And I can't wait to see Bill in a tux. Since he doesn't even like to wear a tie, it should cause quite a stir around town."

Bill chuckled and waved off her comment. "It won't matter what I'm wearing. Everyone will be looking at Lauren and Wes. It's their day."

"Of course." Julia's eyes sparkled. "But I'm still planning to bring my camera and get a picture of you all dressed up like that. Who knows when it will ever happen again?"

"Hey, I get dressed up. I own a very nice suit."

"How many times have you worn it?"

Bill rubbed his chin. "Twice. Once for John and Lisa's wedding and once for their reception."

Julia laughed softly. "That was on the same day, so it only counts as one time, and that was two years ago."

Jenn's stomach tightened. Julia's playful tone hinted at more than friendship between her and Bill. Did Bill feel the same way about Julia?

Surprise stirred her heart. Why was she even considering the question? She wasn't interested in Bill. But she couldn't help watching them and trying to figure out what was going on beneath the surface.

Jenn crossed her arms and felt the scars underneath her

sleeve. She glanced at Julia's smooth, glowing skin, and her heart clenched. She'd never look like that again.

"So, where are you headed?" Julia focused on Bill, a hopeful light in her eyes.

Bill looked past Julia's shoulder. "We're going over to the café to grab some lunch."

Jenn waited, holding her breath. Would he ask Julia to come along?

But he turned to Jenn. "Are you ready?"

She nodded, relief making her feel ten pounds lighter. "Nice to meet you, Julia."

"You, too." Julia lifted her gaze to meet Bill's. "See you Sunday?"

He flashed a warm smile. "I'll be there." Then he placed his hand on Jenn's lower back and with gentle pressure signaled it was time to go. After they took a couple steps, he dropped his hand, and Jenn found herself missing his touch.

She silently scolded herself and reigned in her runaway emotions. Bill was her brother's roommate and her friend. That's all. She wasn't foolish enough to believe he wanted more than that. And even if he did, she couldn't imagine opening her heart or showing him her scars.

CHAPTER 8

"I need to find a job." Jenn twisted the paper napkin in her hands as she looked across the café table at Bill.

Her sudden shift in the conversation took him by surprise. He swallowed a sip of his iced tea and noticed her eyes were a pretty moss green today. He squelched that thought and forced himself to focus. "What kind of job?"

"I'm not sure. I was hoping you could tell me about some of the local businesses, places I might be able to apply."

He nodded slowly, mentally sorting through possibilities in and around Tipton. "What kind of work do you want to do?"

She sent him a rueful smile. "Well, I don't think I'm going to get a job based on my education or training."

"Why not?"

Her cheeks flushed and she leaned forward slightly. "My degree is in performing arts. The only job I've had since graduation was working at a dinner theater. The supporting actors wait on tables before the show, so I suppose I could apply at restaurants."

She glanced around the Wild River Café, watching the

fifty-something waitress approach the neighboring table with a piece of apple pie in one hand and a steaming coffee carafe in the other. "But all I really did was take drink orders and tell people when it was their turn for the buffet." She sighed and turned to stare out the window, a look of discouragement settling over her face.

Bill rubbed his chin. "We have a community theater group, but I'm not sure if the actors are paid or volunteers."

She poked around at her chicken salad without taking a bite. "I don't really want to be on stage right now."

He nodded. Was it her smoke damaged voice or her scars that held her back? He wasn't sure, but either way he imagined it was frustrating to have to give up her career, even temporarily, because of her injuries. "So, what else to you like to do?"

She bit her lower lip for a moment then shifted her gaze back to him. "I like to hunt through flea markets and garage sales looking for hidden treasure." A small smile lifted the corners of her mouth. "Last summer I found an old child's rocker and a small, three-drawer dresser. I refinished and painted them for a friend who was having a baby. She liked them so much she asked me to paint a mural on the wall of the baby's room to match the designs on the furniture."

"What was the mural like?"

"It was a forest scene with fairies, elves and a waterfall." She gazed out the window again, a dreamy look in her eyes. "I totally lost track of time when I was working on it. My friend had to remind me to stop and eat. It took over a week to finish, but she loved it, and so did I."

"So, you're an artist, too."

She smiled. "Well, I've taken a few art classes, and I enjoy creating unique gifts for people, but that was the first time I ever tackled a mural."

An idea formed in his mind. He turned it over for a few

seconds before he made his decision. "How would you like to paint a mural for me?"

Her eyes widened. "I can't imagine a wall filled with fairies at your house."

He grinned. "Me neither. But I can picture a mural with Vermont plants and animals at the nature center. You could make it like a big painting but add the names of the plants and animals so it could be educational as well as artistic."

Her eyes lit up as she listened to him talk. "Are you serious? You'd hire me to paint a mural?"

"Sure. Wes and I were just talking about taking down those old display cases near the entrance. I think a mural would look great there."

Doubt flashed across her expression. "But you haven't seen my work. How do you know I'm good enough?"

"Do you think you can do it?"

She hesitated a moment, then lifted her gaze to meet his. "If we can find pictures of the plants and animals you want me to include, I'm sure I can do it."

Bill nodded, a hope rising in his chest. Not only would he be giving her a job, he'd be helping her tap into different talents that could provide a new focus. "I have a shelf full of books at the nature center. I think you'll find everything you need there."

"Great." Her eyes sparkled now.

"I'm not sure how much we can pay. I'll have to check with Mr. Zeller, but there's money set aside for new displays, so I'm sure we can work something out."

She nodded, grinning like she'd won some prize.

"So, we have a deal?" He held out his hand.

She reached to shake it, her smile radiant. "You just hired yourself an artist."

Jenn dipped her brush in the soft blue paint and stroked across the next section of sky. From her vantage point, four steps up on the sturdy wooden ladder, she glanced at the drawings she'd painstakingly added to the wall over the last few days.

This mural had turned out to be a bigger project than she'd first imagined. With Bill's help, she'd spent a day skimming books and collecting ideas. It took two more days to draw each section of the mural on a large drawing pad. Then she'd spent a couple days transferring the drawings to the wall, much of the time working up on the ladder and stretching to reach several feet away.

This morning she'd driven Wes's car into Richboro and purchased the paint and brushes. Finally, this afternoon, she'd begun to paint, working on the sky and clouds first.

She laid her brush on the tin pie plate she used as a palette and climbed down the ladder. Lifting her gaze, she studied her work, checking to see if the color she had mixed for the sky matched the previous section.

The tense muscles in her neck and back screamed, reminding her that she'd demanded more of them these past few days than she had since the fire. Groaning, she squeezed her shoulder and tried to rub out the pain.

Bill walked toward her. He'd spent the morning teaching a group of boy scouts how to build a rope bridge, and the last time she'd seen him he'd been a muddy mess. Evidently, he'd showered over at the lodge locker room and now wore clean cargo shorts and a dark green Wild River t-shirt, revealing his tanned, muscular arms and legs.

"How's it going? Everything okay?"

"Yes, I'm just a little stiff."

"Where does it hurt?"

She hesitated then pointed to her neck and shoulders. "Guess I'm not used to stretching and painting up on a ladder like that."

He nodded. "I do a lot of hiking and we get sore from carrying our packs. I know what'll help." He stepped behind her and began gently kneading her sore neck muscles.

Jenn tensed, expecting pain as he touched the collar covering the scars on the side of her neck, but the slow, soothing motion of his warm hands felt wonderful. Closing her eyes, she released a deep sigh and let the tension melt away.

"You don't have to push so hard, Jenn," he murmured as he continued the neck massage. "There's no rush with this project."

"I know. But I like what I'm doing. I hate to stop."

He rubbed a little harder, working his way out to her shoulder where her deeper scars were still tender. She winced.

"Sorry, is that too much?" He leaned in closer, and she felt his warm breath on her cheek.

"No, it's good. It's just that my right shoulder is still healing from . . ."

He froze, then dropped his hands. "I'm sorry."

She turned and faced him. "It's okay."

He shifted his gaze to the mural and crossed his arms. A slight frown creased the area between his eyebrows as he silently studied her work.

Regret washed over her. Were her scars always going to put a damper on her relationships and separate her from the people who meant the most to her?

The question shook her. When had she started thinking of Bill like that?

Over the last week they had spent hours together at his house and the nature center. As they poured over books and discussed plans for the mural, she'd stepped into his world and discovered he had extensive knowledge and a deep love for nature. But he kept his feelings about most other things well hidden, at least from her.

Oh, he'd been kind and considerate, being sure she had everything she needed to do her job and feel comfortable at the house. Last Monday he'd spent a couple hours moving his clothes and personal items into the smaller bedroom next to the kitchen, the one he used as on office. He'd insisted she take his larger bedroom upstairs. She resisted, but he wouldn't change his mind.

There'd even been a few times when she sensed he might be interested in deepening their friendship, but then something always seemed to stop him, and he would pull back. Like right now.

"So, what do you think?" She motioned toward the mural and smiled, hoping to draw him back to the closeness they'd shared a few moments ago.

"It looks good." But his expression remained neutral, and he kept his focus on the mural.

Her spirits sagged, and she silently scolded herself. What was she thinking? She didn't want a relationship with Bill or anyone right now. Her future was too up in the air. She pushed those thoughts away and studied her mural again.

"I want to finish up the sky this afternoon and start on those trees on the left."

He turned to her, frowning slightly. "You can call it a day any time you want."

Irritation prickled through her. "I'm okay. I was just taking a little break."

He glanced at his watch. "It's almost three, and you worked through lunch. Why don't you take my truck and head home? I can ride with Wes later."

His concern softened her heart. This was the first time he'd invited her to use his truck, but she didn't want special treatment. She could put in a full day just like anyone else. "Thanks, but I can stay until four."

He sighed and lifted his hands. "Okay." He started to

walk away then turned back. "Hey, what are you doing tonight?"

The question threw her. She blinked and tried to look past his unreadable expression. "I don't know."

"Do you want to come over to Julia's?"

Now she was even more confused. Why would he invite her to Julia's?

"Our small group meets there every other Friday," he continued. "I thought you might like to come along and meet some new friends."

Her stomach tensed. This probably had something to do with the church Bill and Wes attended. "What kind of group is it?"

"Eight of us get together for Bible study. One of the guys brings his guitar. We sing and then pray for each other. It's relaxed, informal. And the first time we meet each month we have dinner together." He smiled and patted his stomach. "Tonight's the night. I can't wait. Julia's a great cook."

Annoyance zinged along her nerves. What about all the meals she'd made? Didn't he consider her a good cook? She squelched the question. "Thanks, but I think I'll pass." She had no intention of discussing her lack of faith in a group—big or small—and she certainly didn't want to be put in a position where her ignorance of the Bible would be painfully obvious to Bill and everyone else.

"Ah, come on." A mischievous look lit up his face. "You don't want to miss this. It'll be fun."

"I have to do my laundry." It was a lame excuse, but she couldn't think of anything else to say.

"You have plenty of time to do laundry after work. We won't get together until seven."

Her face flushed. She shook her head and climbed back up the ladder.

"Come on." He tugged on the leg of her jeans. "Everyone's really nice. I'm sure you'd have a good time."

"No thanks. Not tonight."

He chuckled. "You just need someone to convince you to stop hiding out—"

"I am not hiding!"

He looked up at her, and his teasing expression melted away. "Then what are you doing?"

She gripped the ladder, trying to rein in her surging emotions. "I'm painting the mural you hired me to paint. Then I'm going home to do my laundry."

"Is it the Bible study part that's bothering you? Because if it—"

"No!"

He continued looking at her with a calm steady gaze. "We wouldn't put you on the spot, I promise. You could just listen."

She climbed down, barely holding back her fury. "How many different ways do I have to say this? I am not interested in sitting around and listening to a bunch of people try to convince me that God loves me and has a wonderful plan for my life."

He shook his head slowly. "You don't understand. It's not like that. No one is going to try and talk you into—"

"No, you don't understand." She jabbed her finger at his chest. "When I was fifteen, I prayed my heart out, but my parents died anyway. If God cared anything about me, He would've answered my prayers and kept them alive."

Bill stared at her, a stunned expression on his face.

"He let my apartment burn down, my dog die, and all my friends walk out on me. He left me with nothing. How could I ever trust a loving God like that?"

Pain filled his eyes. "I'm sorry, Jenn," he whispered.

His quiet sympathy did her in. Tears blurred her vision, and she turned and dashed out of the room.

CHAPTER 9

*B*ill trudged into his office and sank into his desk chair. Why hadn't he seen it coming? Jenn obviously wasn't ready to talk about spiritual issues or go to his small group. His timing was totally off. How could he be so dense where women were concerned? Or was it just this one woman who left him feeling stumped and tongue-tied?

No, it was the whole disturbing species!

Wes sat at the corner desk working on the computer, filling in information on the nature center website calendar. He glanced over at Bill. "Hey, what's up?"

"I really blew it with Jenn."

Wes swiveled his chair around. "What do you mean?"

"I asked her to come over to Julia's tonight."

Understanding flickered in Wes's eyes. "And she wasn't ready."

"You got it." Bill clasped his hands. "I shouldn't have pushed her so hard. But I didn't understand what was going on until it was too late, and she blew up."

Wes's eyebrows rose. "What did she say?"

Bill repeated the painful conversation. Then he slouched

in the chair. "She needed answers, but I had no idea what to say."

"I'm not sure she's ready for answers," Wes added. "It sounds like she's still grieving. She's probably stuck in one of those stages."

"What do you mean?"

"The stages of grief. You've heard of them, right?"

Squinting, Bill tried to recall the information he'd learned in his college psychology class several years earlier. "Oh yeah, there's denial, then anger . . ." He rubbed his chin. "Can't remember the rest."

"Bargaining, depression and acceptance." Wes crossed his arms, looking deep in thought. "Even though it's been almost ten years since our parents died, I think she's still holding on to a lot of anger and blaming God. And everything that's happened lately brings it all up again."

"She's definitely upset. I can tell you that. She took off crying." Bill clamped his jaw as he recalled how she'd spun away from him and dashed out the door. He'd gone after her, but stopped when he saw her pacing at the far end of the nature center parking lot. What else could he say? An ocean of grief separated them, and she wasn't willing to reach out to the only source of help he could recommend.

Wes pushed back his chair and stood. "I'll go look for her."

"Yeah, maybe she'll talk to you." Bill wearily rubbed his forehead. Why hadn't he prayed and waited for clear direction instead of plunging ahead on his own? Now it would be even more difficult to have any kind of deeper conversation with her.

Wes slowed as he passed Bill's desk. "Hey, don't beat yourself up. I'm sure it will all work out for the best. At least now we know what she's thinking."

"Yeah, I just wish I knew how to help her." He shook his head. "A few times lately, she seemed more open and willing to talk. But then I freeze up, and I can't put the words together. I know what I believe, but trying to explain it to her is just . . ."

Wes clamped a firm hand on his shoulder. "What you say is important, but the way you live and what you do has a big impact too."

Bill hoped his lifestyle reflected his beliefs, but he wasn't sure that was enough to help Jenn find the answers she needed so desperately.

"You've already done a lot, letting her stay at the house and giving her your room. And getting her this job. Now that was a miracle." Wes focused his gaze on him. "How'd you do that? I thought Mr. Zeller said there was a hiring freeze all summer?"

Bill looked down and flipped through a stack of papers on his desk, trying to ignore Wes's question.

"Bill? Are you funding her position?"

Bill scowled as he pushed back and got up. "Promise me you won't tell her. That would ruin everything."

"You should've said something. I could've helped."

Bill shook his head. "Mr. Zeller liked the idea of the mural—but he wouldn't release the money. I knew Jenn needed a job that paid, so I told him I'd give the money to the nature center, but it had to be used to pay Jenn."

"Man, that's really generous. I appreciate it, and I know Jenn would, too, if she knew."

"Well, don't tell her. Right now she thinks her artwork is worth something, and it is. It's good."

Wes held up his hand. "You don't have to convince me. I'm amazed at what she's done. I always knew she was a talented actress with a beautiful voice, but I had no idea she was so artistic."

"It's going to look great, and when people see it, maybe she'll get some more jobs. There's got to be some other places that need murals."

Wes folded his arms across his chest. "Are you sure you don't want me to help pay—"

"No, you and Lauren have to cover of all the wedding expenses. I have the money. It's not a problem."

Wes smiled and slapped him on the shoulder. "Okay, thanks."

"Don't worry about it." Uneasiness tightened Bill's chest. Did he deserve the trust and appreciation he saw in Wes's eyes? Was he helping Jenn because of the commitment they'd made to try and reach her spiritually, or was something else behind his desire to take care of her and make sure she had a job that might keep her in Vermont?

~

JENN PUSHED OPEN the front door of Bill's house and stepped inside. She glanced around and quietly closed the door behind her.

She'd disappeared from work almost four hours earlier without telling Bill where she was going. Wes had found her in the nature center parking lot and offered to talk, but she wasn't ready. He gave her a hug and told her he loved her. That helped, but she still felt she needed to get away and think things through. He'd offered her the use of his car, and she accepted.

She drove around for a while and then parked at the lake, hoping if she didn't go home until seven, Bill would be gone. Evidently, she hadn't stayed away long enough.

The delicious smell of garlic, herbs, and chicken floated toward her, making her mouth water and empty stomach rumble. With a weary sigh, she gave in and followed the delicious scents into the kitchen.

Bill stood in front of the stove stirring something in a large frying pan. He glanced over his shoulder at her then turned back to the stove and dropped some sliced green peppers and onions into the pan.

Jenn stayed in the doorway, waiting. "I thought you were going over to Julia's."

"We postponed it until next Friday. Lauren and Wes are meeting with Pastor Dan for pre-marital counseling, and Chad is sick."

"Oh." She didn't know Wes and Lauren were in Bill's Bible study group. She walked a little closer. "What are you making?"

"Chicken and ziti."

She watched him add some dried tomatoes to the chicken and vegetables. "Wow, it smells good."

He continued stirring the mixture in the pan, his back to her.

She pulled in another tempting whiff and swallowed. Why wasn't he talking? Was he going to let one argument ruin their friendship? What about all the fun they'd had working together at the nature center? And how about the way they enjoyed kicking back and relaxing at home?

Her empty stomach rumbled as she recalled how she'd dumped her load of frustration and doubts on him, but she quickly forced that memory away.

This was his fault. He had pushed her too far. She couldn't stay here if he was going to pressure her to attend church or get involved in a Bible study group. She wasn't ready, and she might never be.

Of course, this was the first time he had invited her, and he hadn't actually pressured her in a mean way. He was probably just clueless and hadn't sensed her rising frustration until it was too late.

But still, he should know not to tease her about a personal issue like that.

She pressed her lips together. There was no way around it.

She owed him an apology. "I'm sorry I took off today. I just didn't want—"

"No, it's okay." He switched off the burner and turned to face her. "I was out of line. I thought joking around would convince you to come. I didn't know—"

She lifted her hand. "Let's just forget about it. We don't need to get into it now."

He studied her for a moment. "All right. I just have a couple things I want to say."

She steeled herself, preparing for an argument.

He leaned back against the counter. "I've been thinking about what you said. You asked me some tough questions. I believe there are answers for them. But I won't push you, Jenn. I'll leave it up to you to bring them up again when you're ready."

She blinked, stunned by his gentle tone and sincere expression. She'd rarely seen this serious side of Bill. "Okay. Thanks. I appreciate that."

He smiled at her with his slightly crooked grin. "So, are we still friends?"

She smiled and nodded. "Sure."

"You want to try some of my famous Chicken Two Tomato Ziti?"

She laughed. "Yes, I'm starved."

"How about eating out on the deck?"

"Sounds great." She opened the cabinet and pulled out two dinner plates.

Bill's comment about answers to her questions pricked her curiosity. She wasn't ready to talk about them tonight, but she appreciated the way he resolved the tension between them with openness and a calm attitude. That certainly wasn't Phillip's style.

A ripple of surprise passed through her. Why was she comparing Bill and Phillip again?

A few minutes later they sat on the back deck enjoying

Bill's delicious chicken and ziti, freshly steamed broccoli, and crusty Italian bread. Jenn settled back in her chair, soaking in the peaceful evening. The sunset had faded from bright blue to a soft gold. Crickets chirped in a steady chorus, and water tumbled over the rocks in the little stream at the bottom of the hill.

"It's so beautiful here." She watched two squirrels chase each other around the huge trunk of an old oak tree. They chattered and flicked their tails at each other.

"Do you miss Oregon?" Bill took another bite of chicken and watched her.

"I love the Northwest, but Vermont has its own special beauty." She sipped her ice water and set her glass aside. "There is one thing I miss though."

"What's that?"

"Getting up on a high hill and looking down on everything. I've always loved that.

"When I was a little girl, we used to drive up to the top of Mt. Tabor near our home in Portland and look out over the whole city. On a sunny day you can see Mt. Hood and the Columbia and Willamette Rivers. And at night the city lights spread out and sparkle for miles and miles." She smiled at the memory, missing her hometown a little more than she'd realized.

He chuckled. "Sounds nice, but we have all kinds of hills and mountains around here. We're famous for them."

"That's what I've heard, but I've been here almost two weeks, and it seems like everywhere we go we're just driving back and forth in a valley. Even the nature center is at the bottom of the ski slopes. I've never been up high enough to get a good look around."

"There are some great viewpoints on the Round Mountain trail. We should get a group together and go for a hike."

"What's it like?" She set her plate on the small table between them, hoping she wouldn't have to tell him she'd never been hiking before. He was such an outdoorsman. She didn't want him to laugh at her and think she was a wimpy city girl.

"It's about four miles long, there's a bit of a climb, but most of it is pretty level. Great views. You'd love it."

She imagined herself hiking down a trail with Bill, enjoying the scenic beauty of Vermont. "Sounds great."

His smile spread wider, delight filling his eyes. "You really want to go?"

She felt heat stealing into her face. "Sure."

"Okay, I'll see if I can get some people together. Maybe Wes and Lauren will come. I think Toby might even be able to do this hike. I'll check with Wes and see what he says."

As soon as Bill mentioned pulling a group together, a tempting thought struck her. "What about Julia?" Jenn watched Bill's face, trying to gauge his reaction to the suggestion.

He lifted his dark eyebrows. "I suppose we could ask her. She hasn't come on too many hikes with us, but we all went fishing on Stillwater Lake last month and she was a good sport. At least she wasn't like some girls, squealing at every bug that flies by or afraid to bait her own hook." Bill chuckled and shook his head.

Jenn nodded and determined she would prove she could hike up mountains, battle bugs, and bait hooks with the best of them, or at least as well as Julia.

CHAPTER 10

*J*enn glanced out her bedroom window across the wildflower-filled front yard and checked the sky. The weather looked perfect for hiking. She smiled and trotted down the steps, her heart as light as the fluffy clouds she'd seen overhead. When she reached the living room, she grabbed two dirty coffee cups off the end table and carried them into the kitchen.

Wes stood near the sink, the phone to his ear, his head bent in concentration. "Does he have a fever?" He paced toward the sliding glass door leading to the back deck, a frown creasing his forehead as he listened. "Okay. I'll be right over. We can decide what to do then." He walked back to the counter and hung up the phone.

Jenn set the cups in the sink. "Who's sick?"

"Lauren's been up all night with Toby. He can't keep anything down. She's trying to decide if she should take him to the doctor. And Christy, the girl who works with her in the gallery, is late again." He shook his head. "That's the second time this week."

"So, you're going over there to help?"

"Yeah. I can fill in until Christy shows up or give Lauren a hand with Toby." He sighed and shook his head. "Poor little guy. Sounds like he's really miserable."

Bill walked into the kitchen carrying his backpack. "Morning. You guys about ready to head out?"

Wes explained Lauren's call and Toby's illness. "Lauren and I need to stick around home today."

"Sorry Toby's sick." Bill pulled his water bottle and a bag of nuts out of the backpack and set them on the counter.

Jenn sank into a kitchen chair. First Julia had canceled because some people from out of town had called and asked to see properties for sale in Tipton. Now Wes and Lauren couldn't go.

Wes grabbed his toast off the counter. "Hey, that doesn't mean you guys have to cancel the hike."

Bill glanced uncertainly at Wes.

"It's a beautiful day." Wes gestured to the sliding glass door. "Why don't you get out there and enjoy it?"

Bill shifted his focus to Jenn. "Do you still want to go?"

Her stomach did a funny little flip. Would that be weird for just the two of them to go? Wouldn't that be almost like a date? No, she was being silly. She'd been looking forward to this hike all week. The mural was finished, and she wanted to get out of the house and celebrate. She smiled at him. "I'm up for it if you are."

Some undefined emotion flickered in Bill's eyes. "Okay. Let's get our gear together, and we can head out."

An hour later, after dropping Wes off at Lauren's and making a quick stop at the Green Mountain Bakery for blueberry cake donuts and coffee, they arrived at the trailhead where they planned to leave Bill's truck and begin their hike.

"I'm glad you suggested leaving Wes's car where the trail ends." Jenn climbed out of the truck and bent to tie her shoelace. "Hiking four miles one-way sounds a lot better to me than doing an eight-mile round-trip back here."

Grinning, Bill grabbed their packs from the back of the

truck and handed the smaller blue one to her. "Well, I want you to enjoy this hike, not get blisters and sore feet."

His comment made her smile, and she felt all the more determined to meet this new challenge head on. She'd show Bill she was not a prissy city girl, but someone who could hike through the woods and enjoy nature with him. She slipped the backpack on and tugged her shirt back in place.

Bill leaned in closer and helped her adjust the straps. "You want this to ride a little higher on your shoulders or you'll get uncomfortable."

She caught a whiff of his clean, woodsy aftershave and pulled in a deep breath.

"How's that?" He lifted his gaze to meet hers. His eyes looked very blue today with little specks of gray around the iris.

Blushing, she tore her gaze away and silently scolded herself for gawking at him. "It's . . . fine." The pack actually rubbed on her sore shoulder, so she shifted it a little, thankful she only carried her lunch and Wes's camera.

"Okay. Let's go." Bill turned and led the way toward the trail, walking at an easy pace.

Jenn followed him and shifted her attention to the quiet, shady forest. They walked along in silence for a few minutes until Jenn asked Bill about a particular tree with a huge, rough trunk.

He told her it was a red oak and launched off on a two-minute spiel, giving her the all the details. He slowed and glanced over his shoulder. "Sorry, just throw a stick at me if I get too boring."

She laughed. "You're not boring. I like learning about the trees up here. Most of these are different from what we have in Oregon." She walked on studying the tall ferns growing at the side of the trail. The fronds curled in a perfect circle reminding her of lush feathers.

She took another step and winced. "Hold on just a

second." She sat on a fallen log covered with moss and reached to untie her shoe.

Bill turned back. "What's the matter?"

"I think I've got a rock in my shoe."

"Let me help." He knelt in front of her and loosened her shoelace.

"Thanks." She felt a little like Cinderella as he pulled off her shoe, shook out the rock, and then slipped it back on.

He tied it and looked up at her. "How's that?"

She stood and took a couple steps. "Feels much better. Thanks."

They walked on, treading through a patch of soft pine needles covering the forest floor. A pair of cute little chipmunks raced across their path and scuttled up a tree.

Jenn spotted a trillium plant with its white, three-petaled flower above three broad leaves just like one she'd painted in the mural and pointed it out to Bill.

He chuckled. "You have a very good memory."

"Painting that mural was a great way for me to learn about the plants and animals around here."

They rounded a curve and Jenn gasped with delight. The forest fell away on one side of the trail, opening up to a beautiful view of Wild River Valley below them. "Wow, I didn't realize we were up so high."

Bill stood at her side, obviously enjoying her reaction.

Jenn lifted her hand and shaded her eyes as she took in the view. "What's the name of that lake?" She pointed to the far end of the valley where the silver water shimmered in the morning sunlight.

He stepped up behind her and leaned in close to see where she was pointing. "That's Jarmen Lake, one of the best spots for canoeing around here. Good fishing too. It has some great little islands you can explore out in the middle."

His breath tickled her cheek and sent a delightful shiver through her. She glanced over her shoulder at him. Their gazes connected and held. She sent him a tremulous smile and turned back to the view of the valley. But all her senses focused in on him, savoring his nearness.

Bill stepped away and crossed his arms. A slight frown replaced his smile, and he stared silently into the distance.

Disappointment lodged in her heart. He didn't like being close to her. She could feel it. Reaching up, she touched her collar. Had the straps of her backpack pulled her shirt away from her neck and exposed her scars? Anguish twisted through her at that thought. She tried to focus on the view, but her thoughts jumped back to Bill. Was he repulsed by what he'd seen? Was that why he moved away and always seemed to raise a wall between them whenever he got close?

Stop! It didn't matter what Bill thought of her. She didn't want to get involved with him. That would be too complicated and painful. And she definitely couldn't deal with any more pain or complications in her life right now.

They hiked on for another hour then stopped to take a break and eat lunch at the next viewpoint. Bill lounged in the shade on a soft bed of pine needles. She sat a few feet away with her back against a large rock, looking out over the Valley. Wild River curled through the forest below them like a twisted silver ribbon. She followed its path as far as she could see and wondered if it eventually emptied into Lake Champlain.

A strong breeze rustled through the trees overhead and blew Jenn's hair in her face. She swiped it out of her eyes and glanced over at Bill.

He sat up and scanned the sky, then stood and brushed off his pants. Frowning, he studied the thick clouds gathering behind them in the west. "Looks like it's going to rain."

Another gust of wind blew past, turning the leaves over. The birds fell silent, and a strange quietness settled over the forest. Thunder rumbled in the distance.

Goosebumps rose on Jenn's arms. "Should we turn back?"

Bill searched the sky again. "We're over halfway. We need to keep going."

Her stomach muscles tightened as she thought of getting caught in a storm. A surge of wind whipped through the trees. It swirled around them, stirring up a cloud of dried leaves and pine needles. She squinted and shielded her face against the flying debris.

Bill grabbed her hand. "Come on. I don't like the look of this. We need to get out of the open." They dashed down the trail and back into the woods just as huge raindrops began pelting them.

"There are some caves up ahead," Bill called over his shoulder. "We can get out of the rain there."

Jenn's heart raced as she leaped over rocks and fallen logs. The shower became a downpour, and soon they were soaked to the skin and splashing through mud puddles.

"Up here." Bill took her hand again and led her off the trail, over some slippery rocks, and into a large opening in the hillside shrouded by thick brush and tall trees.

Jenn stumbled into the cave, panting from their mad dash. She swiped her hand across her wet face and pushed her hair out of her eyes. Water ran down her legs, into her socks, and dripped onto the dusty ground at her feet. Her clothes clung to her, sending a clammy shiver down her back. Cool air carrying a dank, musty scent drifted toward her from the deep recesses of the cave.

"Man, that's some storm." Bill wiped his eyes and shook off his hands. Rain had plastered his dark hair to his forehead, and little rivulets ran down his face and dripped off his chin. He reached for his shoulder straps and pulled off his backpack. "I've got an extra shirt we can use like a towel."

Jenn reached for her straps and froze. "Oh no, I left my backpack at the viewpoint."

Still breathing deeply, Bill glanced toward the mouth of

the cave. Outside, rain poured down like a hose on full blast. "You've got your camera in there, don't you?"

"Wes's camera, actually." How could she have left it behind? Why hadn't she been more careful?

"I'll get it." As he turned to leave, thunder rumbled again. It sounded miles away, but closer than the first time they'd heard it.

"Wait!" She grabbed his arm. "You can't go back out there."

"It'll only take a few minutes, and most of the way I'm under a lot of trees, not out in the open."

"But . . ." She bit her quivering lip.

He reached out and gently ran his fingers down the side of her face. "Don't worry. I'll be all right."

Surprised by his tender touch, she blinked and watched him head back out into the storm.

CHAPTER 11

Bill snatched Jenn's backpack off the ground and stuffed it under his shirt. No time to check it now. Lightning flashed, and about two seconds later a loud crack split the air followed by a stunning explosion of thunder. The ground shook, and he took off running down the trail. The storm was traveling faster than he expected. He shot off a prayer for mercy, knowing full well he was breaking almost every lightning safety rule he'd ever been taught.

He sprinted over the muddy trail, panting, and promising himself he would never do anything this stupid again. Lightning flashed overhead, but he continued his mad dash along the tree-lined path. Finally, he scaled the slippery granite boulders and climbed toward the opening in the hillside where he'd left Jenn.

Thunder exploded behind him as he ducked inside the cave. Pulling in a ragged breath, he dropped the backpack and searched for Jenn. His eyes quickly adjusted to the dim light, and he spotted her crouched against the far wall, her hands over her ears and her eyes squeezed shut. One look at her frightened, pale face and he knew he shouldn't have left her.

He called her name as he walked toward her, but the rumbling thunder overpowered his voice. He touched her shoulder, and her eyes flew open. The raw fear he saw there cut him to the heart. "Hey, it's okay."

He reached for her, and she leaped into his embrace. He tucked her in close and ran his hand down her damp hair, hoping to still her trembling. "It's all right. You're safe in here."

Thunder crashed again beyond the cave entrance. She cringed, and her whole body tensed.

He held her close until the rumble faded, then pulled back and looked into her face. "The thunder can't hurt you."

She averted her gaze. "I know, I just don't like the sound of it."

He gently brushed a wet strand of hair off her cheek, trying to think of a way to distract her from the storm.

"When I was a little kid, I used to get really scared during thunderstorms." He shifted so he could see her face better. "My dad would joke around and tell me the angels were bowling up in heaven. If it was dark, we'd turn off all the lights and watch the lightning flash. He made it fun, like a party. I guess that was his way of trying to help me get over my fears." He chuckled, remembering his dad's love for life and sense of humor. "Guess it worked. I like a good storm now." He lifted his eyebrows and sent her a teasing grin.

"Well I don't." She pulled away and paced to the far side of the cave, clutching her folded arms across her chest.

A wave of regret swamped his heart. When was he going to learn that joking and making light of Jenn's fears was not the way to reach her heart? He ran his hand through his wet hair. "I'm sorry. I shouldn't be teasing you about something that scares you."

She turned back toward him, a silent apology in her expression. "No, it's not your fault. I just . . ." She closed her eyes for a moment, then she straightened and focused on him.

"Every time I hear the thunder, I feel like I'm hearing my apartment explode all over again." As if her words brought it on, thunder cracked and boomed overhead, and she raised her hands to her ears.

No wonder she hated the storm. He crossed the distance between them and took her in his arms once more. Closing his eyes, he prayed for the right words to comfort her. There had to be something he could say, but no answer came. So he held her, hoping his presence and strength would be enough to absorb some of the bad memories.

Together, they waited for the thunder's fury to fade. She rested her head against his chest, her tense muscles finally relaxing. He slowed his breathing to match hers and listened as the sound of the rain grew softer.

She shifted slightly and looked up at him. This time warmth glowed in her shimmering green eyes. Her cheeks were damp from hugging him, and water drops laced her eyelashes.

Looking into her lovely face, his heartbeat sped up like he was running down the trail again. He pulled in a deep, shaky breath. She smelled fresh like mountain flowers and summer rain. Only a few inches separated them now. If he leaned down he could kiss her, and the sweet invitation in her eyes said she would welcome him.

But a voice he knew well spoke to his heart. *Don't take what isn't yours. She needs a Savior, and you are not Him.*

The truth pierced his conscience and cleared his thinking. If he kissed her now it would send them down a path to heartache, a path they would both regret. Groaning inwardly, he broke his gaze, and let his hands drop.

Her lips parted, confusion flickered in her eyes, and she took a step back.

Regret filled his chest and almost knocked the wind out of him. It was too late. Their time together today had deepened their connection and started them down that path, and there was no way to pretend it hadn't happened.

~

JENN CLOSED THE FRONT DOOR, lowered her soggy backpack to the floor, and kicked off her muddy shoes. Trudging toward the kitchen she wondered which hurt more—her sore leg muscles, her tired feet, or her aching heart.

What was going on with Bill? One minute he was gentle and caring, taking her in his arms like a rescuing hero, and the next he was cool and detached, acting as though he wished she wasn't around. It didn't make sense.

For a moment, back in the cave, she thought he was going to kiss her. She shook her head, certain she must have imagined it. How embarrassing! At least she hadn't closed her eyes and puckered up. She grimaced and pulled a glass from the cabinet.

Wes stood in front of the open fridge. "How was the hike?"

"Don't ask," she grumbled.

"Hmm, that good?"

She sent him a withering glance and filled her glass from the tap.

"Sorry." He walked over and fingered a strand of her still damp hair. "You guys must've got caught in the rain."

She nodded and took a long drink of cool water. How much should she tell her brother? Maybe if she talked it over with him he could help her figure things out. But she didn't want to put him in the awkward position of choosing between loyalty to her and his best friend.

"Where's Bill?"

"Outside cleaning up his truck." *Probably trying to find a way to avoid being in the same room with me.*

"Let's sit down. I've got something I want to talk to you

about." Wes took a seat at the table and motioned for her to sit across from him.

She settled into the chair and set her glass on the table.

"Lauren wants to offer you a job at her gallery."

Jenn sat up. "Really?"

He nodded. "She had to fire Christy. She's been late several times, and today we found out she's been stealing money from the register."

"Wow, she seemed so nice."

"Yeah, we thought so, too. At least we figured it out before she got away with too much." Wes leaned back in his chair. "Lauren confronted her. She gave some of it back and promised to repay the rest, so we're not going to contact the police."

Jenn nodded and took another drink.

"Lauren needs to hire someone she can trust. She's hoping you'll accept the job so she has time to train you before everything gets too crazy with the wedding."

Wes lifted his hands, his expression apologetic. "I know it's not an acting job, but if you could just commit to stay until we get back from our honeymoon, that would help us out a lot."

"I love the gallery, and working with Lauren would be great."

Wes smiled. "So, you'll talk to Lauren about it?"

"Sure, I'd be crazy to say no to this." She got up and trotted around to the other side of the table and gave her brother a big hug. "Thanks, Wes."

He hugged her back. "Hey, you're the one who would be doing us a favor."

"Well, I appreciate it." Jenn returned to her chair, her mind whirling with possibilities and questions about her new job.

Wes leaned forward, his expression serious. "I need to talk to you about something else, too."

"Okay." She felt a nervous flutter in her stomach.

"What do you think of moving over to Long Meadow and staying with Lauren?"

His question jolted her. "You don't want me to stay here anymore?"

He reached across the table and touched her hand. "I like having you here. But I spend most of my time at Lauren's. And the closer it gets to the wedding, the more we're going to need your help."

Relief rushed in, replacing her fears. He wasn't trying to get rid of her. He wanted her close by, so she could take part in the wedding preparations. Those thoughts wrapped around her heart like a warm blanket. "Okay. Do you think Lauren and Tilley will mind?"

"It was Lauren's idea, and Tilley says it's fine."

Bill walked into the kitchen, his damp hair sticking up and his boots leaving muddy tracks on the tile floor.

Wes chuckled when he saw him. "Man, you look like you fought a battle."

Bill looked down at his clothes. "Yeah, we got caught in a serious storm." He dropped a couple of dirty towels on the floor beside the washing machine. Turning away, he peeled off his dirt-streaked t-shirt.

Jenn's eyes widened as she stared at his broad, muscular shoulders and tanned back.

He dropped the shirt on the floor and then pulled off his hiking boots and socks. Pushing the boots aside, he scooped up the dirty clothes and tossed them in the washing machine. "Do you want to throw anything in?" He turned and faced Jenn.

Her cheeks flamed, and she quickly shifted her gaze away. "No, not right now."

He grabbed the detergent off the shelf, poured a capful into the machine, and adjusted the dials.

Wes tilted back his chair. "Hey, Bill, Jenn's going to be

moving over to Long Meadow and working with Lauren in the gallery."

Bill turned around and leveled his cool blue gaze at her. His left eyebrow rose a fraction. "When did you decide that?"

Jenn swallowed and struggled to find her voice. "Just now."

"Is that what you want?"

She lifted her chin, meeting his silent challenge. "I need a job, and staying with Lauren makes sense." Why did she feel like she had to defend her decision?

Wes grinned, obviously unaware of the undercurrent between Bill and Jenn. "Yeah, now you can have your room back . . . and it's even clean."

Bill scowled at Wes and then stalked off toward his temporary bedroom just off the kitchen. As soon as he crossed the threshold, he jerked the door closed.

Wes rubbed his chin. "What's up with him?" He shifted his focus to Jenn and drummed his fingers on the table. "Did you two have a fight or something?"

Jenn felt her face heating up again. "Not really."

"Well, what's going on then?"

She got up and headed for the stairs. "I have no idea. Why don't you ask Bill?"

CHAPTER 12

*J*enn ran her hand over the soft green and peach quilt covering the queen size bed in her new room at Long Meadow. Even though she'd only worked in Lauren's gallery for five days, she knew the beautiful design and intricate stitching made the quilt worth several hundred dollars.

Her gaze traveled around the room, taking in the sheer peach curtains fluttering in the warm breeze at the window. A tall oak armoire stood in one corner, and on the opposite side of the room sat a matching four-drawer dresser. They gave her more than enough room for the few items of clothing she owned.

Her heart warmed as she thought of all Tilley and Lauren had done to make this room special for her. But more important than that, they treated her like one of the family, and that was something she hadn't experienced in a very long time.

There was only one small wrinkle in the situation—she hadn't seen Bill since the day after their hike when she'd packed her one bag and moved to Long Meadow.

Biting her lip, she glanced toward the open window. What was Bill doing this morning? Was he canoeing in Jarmen Lake or teaching a class at the nature center? Maybe he was having lunch in town with Julia. She pushed those thoughts away, scolding herself for even wondering about it. It was silly to miss him. There was nothing between them.

Moving to Long Meadow was the right choice. Her friendship with Lauren had blossomed as they worked together in the gallery and relaxed at home in the evenings. Wedding plans were the constant topic of conversation, and Jenn loved being right in the middle of it all . . . if only it didn't mean never seeing Bill.

"Jenn, can you come here?" Lauren called from down the hall.

"I'm coming." Jenn stowed away her thoughts of Bill and hurried toward Lauren's bedroom. She pushed open the door, and her mouth dropped open.

Lauren stood in front of the full-length mirror wrapped in a long, white sheet, wearing her floor-length bridal veil, and balancing on one foot.

"What are you doing?" Jenn covered her mouth to stifle a giggle.

"I'm trying to decide which shoe looks better. Lauren lifted one foot as she balanced on the other. "The satin open-toe?" She switched feet. "Or the beaded pump?" Tilting her head to one side, Lauren studied her reflection in the mirror. "What do you think?

"I like the satin open-toe, but what's with the sheet?"

"Oh." Lauren looked down at herself. "Well, my dress is still at the shop being altered, so I thought the sheet would have the same affect and give me an idea of how the shoes would look."

Jenn pressed her lips together, but when Lauren glanced over at her again, she couldn't hold back her laughter. "I'm sorry, but you look so goofy all wrapped up in the sheet like that."

Lauren planted her hand on her hips. "You're a lot of

help!" But she dissolved into laughter along with Jenn, and they flopped down on Lauren's bed.

"I think you should show Wes your lovely gown." Jenn scooted up and sat against the pillows at the head of the bed.

"Go ahead and laugh. Just remember, I'll be the one throwing the bouquet."

"Oh, no!" Jenn put on a mock-horrified expression. She wasn't looking forward to that part of the reception. Would she have to join the group of single women vying for the bouquet, or would she be able to hide out and avoid the embarrassing crush?

Lauren kicked off her mismatched shoes, rolled over, and rested her chin on her palm. She smiled at Jenn with shining eyes. "You know, I'm crazy about your brother."

Jenn nodded. "I think he's very lucky to find someone special like you."

"You're sweet to say that." Lauren's smile faded a little. "But I'm sure he could have picked someone with a lot less baggage and had an easier time."

"The past is history. He loves you. That's all that matters."

Lauren smiled as she pushed her veil over her shoulder. "Thanks. You sound a lot like your brother."

Jenn drew her knees up to her chest and wrapped her arms around her legs. "I wish I was more like him."

Lauren glanced at the photo of Wes on the nightstand and her gaze softened. "I owe Wes so much. If he hadn't come into my life when he did, I don't know what would've have happened to me and Toby."

Wes had told Jenn how he'd met Lauren. He'd been hiking toward Mad River Resort in a snowstorm when Lauren drove by and almost hit a deer that dashed across the road. She'd crashed into a snowbank, and Wes had come to her rescue. But Jenn had always suspected there was more to the story. "Why do you say that?"

Lauren shifted her gaze back to Jenn. "When I first met

your brother, I was carrying a load of guilt and shame that God never intended me to carry. Wes helped me understand God's forgiveness, and he showed me how God can take even the hard and painful things that happen to us and turn them around for good." A gentle smile lifted her mouth. "That's an amazing gift."

Jenn shifted and adjusted the pillows behind her back. She usually felt uncomfortable when someone started talking about God, but this time, Lauren's words soundly strangely appealing. "What do you mean about God turning bad things into good?"

Lauren sat up and faced Jenn. "I've been wanting to tell you about Toby and his father."

"Oh, you don't have to explain anything to me." Jenn fiddled with the hem of her shirt.

"I know, but I want to." She waited until Jenn looked up. "When I was in high school, I had a crush on a boy named Stephen Zeller. We were about as opposite as you could imagine. I was serious and quiet, interested in art and reading, and a good student. He was a cocky, good-looking daredevil. When I was twenty, I came home from college on spring break, and he asked me out."

"I've heard that name before. Is he part of the family who owns Wild River?"

"Yes, Stephen's father, Arthur Zeller owns the resort and the nature center."

Jenn nodded. She'd met Arthur Zeller while she worked on the mural. He was about sixty with a powerful presence, and he seemed to take a hands-on approach to running the resort. And as far as she could tell, he was well respected by everyone who worked there.

"He had two sons, Stephen and Ryan," Lauren continued. "But Stephen died in a skiing accident about a year and a half ago."

"Oh . . . I'm sorry." Jenn studied Lauren's face. Had she loved Stephen Zeller?

"We only dated that one week." A sorrowful look filled Lauren's face. "I didn't really know him very well . . . but he's Toby's father."

Jenn's stomach tightened.

"The night before I was supposed to go back to college I went to a party at Wild River with Stephen. I wanted to fit in, so when Stephen offered me a drink, I took it. A few minutes later I started feeling sick. I'm pretty sure he put something in my drink. I don't remember anything after that until I woke up the next morning still at Wild River. Two months later I found out I was pregnant with Toby."

"Oh, Lauren, that's awful." Jenn had read articles about date rape, but she'd never known anyone who had gone through it. "I'm so sorry that happened to you."

"Thanks." Lauren reached over and squeezed Jenn's hand. "It was a difficult experience. But God took the pain and heartache and eventually brought good things out of them. Being pregnant and alone motivated me to search for a relationship with God, and through some caring friends, I found Him. He gave me an easy pregnancy and a beautiful, healthy son. He took care of us and provided what we needed through a church we attended in Boston.

"Then, last year, after I heard about Stephen's death, I felt I could move home to Tipton. The timing was right. Toby was turning six and needed to start first grade, and Tilley missed us and needed more help. I received a small inheritance from my father's estate, giving me enough money to renovate the barn and open the gallery. I'd just been back for a few months when Wes came to town."

"Wow, that's quite a story."

"Oh, that's just the short version." Lauren laughed. "I'll tell you the whole thing sometime. But what's most important to me is seeing how God's timing and plan are perfect. He brought Wes and me together, and we were able to help each other work through some important issues. It's so awesome now to look back and see what God has done."

Wes had told her similar things about God arranging circumstances and caring for him many times. But for some reason, hearing it from Lauren touched a place deep in her heart. "I used to believe in God," she said, her voice soft and wistful.

"What happened?"

Jenn was quiet for a moment, considering Lauren's honesty and all she had shared. Maybe she'd finally found someone who would listen and understand.

She raised her gaze and met Lauren's. "I guess when God didn't answer my prayers, it hurt too much, so I closed my heart and stopped believing."

Lauren nodded, her eyes full of compassions. "Well, He's still there, and He's never stopped loving you. He's waiting to welcome you home again."

Jenn blinked to clear her vision, pondering that thought for a moment. God waited for her to return? That didn't seem right. Why would He want anything to do with her when she had turned away from Him for so long?

Lauren reached over to her nightstand and picked up a Bible. "This is God's love letter. Why not read it and see what He has to say?"

Jenn hesitated, feeling foolish. "I wouldn't know where to start."

Lauren opened the cover and flipped through the pages. "Start here, in the Gospel of John. It tells the story of Jesus' life from his best friend's perspective." She pulled out a navy-blue satin ribbon that matched the color of Bible's worn leather cover and marked the page. Then she closed the book and offered it to her.

How could she say no? Lauren's gentle yet persuasive words grabbed her heart. Could she find the answers to her questions there? Did she have the courage to try? Lauren seemed to believe this was what she needed, and that was enough to make her reach out and take the Bible from Lauren's hand.

∼

Bill unlocked the front door and pushed it open. Gripping his keys and backpack in one hand, he grabbed the two bags of groceries with the other and trudged into his dark, quiet house.

A terrible smell overwhelmed him as he entered the kitchen. Searching the counters and sink, he spotted the same pile of dirty dishes he'd left there this morning. Leaning forward, he sniffed. That didn't' seem to be the source of the foul odor.

He dropped the bags on the floor by the kitchen table, walked across the room, pulled open the shades, and pushed back the sliding glass door. The warm breeze floated in and diluted the stale smell. Glancing over his shoulder, he spotted the overflowing trashcan at the end of the counter. There was the trouble. He'd thrown out some old food from the refrigerator last night, but he had forgotten to take the trash outside.

He gulped in some fresh air then held his breath as he turned and walked back to take care of it. Yanking out the trash bag, he quickly tied it closed and headed out the sliding glass door.

"Man, this stinks," he muttered. Coming home to a dark, empty house every day was getting to him. Although Wes was officially still his roommate, he rarely saw him after work since he spent most evenings at Lauren's.

Over the last two weeks he'd slowly seen his life slip back to his old solitary pattern. No one greeted him when he came home. No one asked him about his day, and no one was around to share a meal or watch a video or listen to music. He lived alone. All alone. And it stunk.

Bill dropped the bag in the large outdoor trashcan and slammed the lid. So, what was he going to do about it? He couldn't look for another roommate until after the wedding and Wes moved out. But it wasn't Wes he missed the most. It was Jennifer.

Bill climbed the steps to the deck and plopped down in a chair. Propping his feet up on the railing, he gazed into the forest. What was Jennifer doing right now? Probably sitting down to a delicious dinner with Tilley, Wes, Lauren, and Toby around the big table in the dining room at Long Meadow. His stomach growled at the thought. There'd be laughter and interesting conversation that would last well over an hour as everyone shared stories about the events of the day.

He heaved a heavy sigh. What was the matter with him? He'd lived by himself for over three years before Wes arrived last January. But once again, he realized it wasn't Wes he was thinking about tonight.

He lifted his eyes to the azure sky above the treetops. *Father, You know how I feel about Jenn, but I made a commitment to you a long time ago. If I'm going to date someone seriously, she has to love You and want to grow spiritually. Jenn definitely isn't there right now, and I have no idea if she ever will be.*

He sighed and rubbed his forehead. *Please soften Jenn's heart. Help her see who You really are and how much You love her. I'm not sure if you can use me in that process. I seem to be messing things up more than helping, but if you want me to be there for her, I'm willing.*

CHAPTER 13

*J*enn stepped into the shade of the blue tarp tent and glanced around at second-hand items on display. The Tipton Flea Market was a treasure trove for the experienced bargain hunter, and Jenn considered herself one of the best.

Since her teenage years she'd enjoyed shopping at thrift stores and garage sales. When she moved into her own apartment, she'd furnished it in eclectic-vintage style with treasures she'd purchased for a song.

Today, Lauren had sent her to the flea market looking for unique items they could use in displays at the gallery. So far, she'd found a wooden tray she hoped to refinish, an unusual willow basket, and eight old leather-bound books.

This booth looked promising with several tables of dishes and decorative glass as well as a few pieces of wooden furniture at the back. Maybe she'd find something truly valuable hidden among the junk and be able to surprise Lauren.

She spotted an old wooden pie safe painted an awful aqua blue and made her way toward it. It stood about five feet tall and about forty inches wide. The chipped and peeling paint would have to go, but underneath she suspected she'd find beautiful wood. She ran her hand over the decorative design punched in one of the front tin panels and admired the repeated heart pattern.

"That's a real beauty." A man wearing a beige hat decorated with several fishing lures stepped forward. His proud stance announced he was the owner of the pie safe and all the other second-hand treasures on display. "That's a genuine antique, not one of those shoddy reproductions," he added with a lift of his gray eyebrows.

"Yes, I can see that." She reached for the drawer handle. "Mind if I take a peek?"

"No, go right ahead." He stepped back, watching her, his old brown eyes alight with interest.

She pulled open the drawer and inspected the inside. The dovetail corners looked sturdy and well made. The tin panels were in good condition with only a few minor dents. Lauren had a similar piece in the gallery, and though this one was smaller, she knew if it were refinished it would be worth three to four hundred, maybe more. She looked up and caught the vendor's eye. "How much are you asking?"

He squinted and pressed his lips together. "Well, I don't think I can let it go for less than three hundred."

Jenn released a wistful sigh. So much for finding a bargain. The man obviously knew the value of antiques.

"Come on, Denny, you know it's not worth half that much."

Jenn turned and found Bill standing behind a few feet away. A dizzy current raced through her. How long had he been there? Evidently long enough to catch her conversation about the pie safe.

Bill winked then moved closer and ran his hand along the peeling paint on the top edge. "It's all scratched up. She'd have to refinish it."

Denny chuckled. "What are you trying to do? Run me out of business?"

Bill retuned a lazy grin. "No, I'm just not sure Jenn knows she's supposed to dicker with you."

"She's a friend of yours?"

"Yes, she is, so you better treat her right." Bill turned to her. "Jennifer Evans, this is Denny Tremont, owner of The Second Time Around in West Harmon."

Jenn smiled and shook Denny's hand. "Nice to meet you."

"Same here." He crossed his arms and studied her with a serious gaze. "Now, if you want the pie safe, you have to make me a counteroffer."

Jenn bit her lip, trying to figure out the game. "Well, I only have—"

Bill held up his hand. "First rule in dickering—never tell him how much you have."

Though she liked to shop for bargains, she didn't like to haggle with anyone over the price. She sent Bill a questioning look.

"You're supposed to make him an offer that's lower than you're willing to pay, knowing you'll have to come up a little as he comes down."

Jenn mentally counted the money in her pocket then shifted her gaze to Denny. "I'll give you a hundred dollars."

Denny laughed. "You're kidding, right? No way will I let it go for less than two hundred and fifty."

That stopped her for a moment. Then she realized she'd made Denny come down fifty dollars, and she grinned at Bill. Straightening her shoulders, she focused on Denny. "It's going to take me a long time to scrape off that old paint. And it'll cost a lot to buy the supplies I need to refinish it. I don't think I want to pay more than one seventy-five."

Denny studied her and rubbed his chin. "Well, since you're a friend of Bill's I could come down to two twenty-five, but that's as low as I'm gonna' go."

Jenn glanced at Bill. She didn't have that much. Was that the end of the game?

"Come on, Denny, why don't you give the lady a deal?"

Denny lifted his hat and rubbed his hand over his shiny, bald head. "Oh, all right. Two hundred, but I must be crazy to let it go for that price."

Jenn reached in her pocket and pulled out all the money she had. "I can give you one seventy-five, but that's all I've got."

"That's a good deal, Denny. You get the cash, and you won't have to haul that heavy thing home this afternoon."

Denny lowered his gaze to the cash in her hand. "Okay, you can have it for one seventy-five."

"Thanks." She turned to Bill and found him grinning, a look of approval in his eyes. "I never dickered for anything before," she said with a little laugh.

Behind her, Denny groaned.

"You better just pay the man before he changes his mind. We can gloat over your victory later."

Jenn turned to Denny and counted the bills into his hand. But when she reached one hundred fifty-five, she ran out of cash. Her face flushed and embarrassment coursed through her. "I'm sorry, I thought for sure I had one seventy-five."

Denny scowled and quickly recounted the money.

She felt perspiration gathering on her cheeks as she watched him.

"One fifty-five." Denny leveled his perturbed gaze at her.

Bill pulled a twenty from his shirt pocket and handed it to him. "One seventy-five."

Denny's expression immediately softened. "Oh, you two were just trying to get me riled up. You had the money all the time."

She opened her mouth to protest.

But Bill stopped her with a little shake of his head. "Will you hold on to the pie safe while we finish shopping?"

"Sure thing. I'll be here until two."

Bill placed his hand at the small of her back and guided

her out of the tent. "You're quite the negotiator," he said, bending close so only she could hear. They stepped into the sun, and he dropped his hand.

She wished he hadn't, then quickly told herself she was making too much out of the caring gesture. She needed to stop imagining there was more than friendship on his mind. "Thanks for bailing me out."

"It's okay." They walked slowly down the aisle passing a booth filled with tools, fishing gear, and hubcaps.

"I'll pay you back on Friday."

He shook his head. "Don't worry about it."

"But I'll have the money then."

He stepped in the shade of the next tent and turned to her. "What do you plan to do with the pie safe?"

"I thought I'd refinish it and try to sell it at the gallery. I've been refinishing and painting designs on some smaller pieces."

"Really?"

She nodded. "So far I've finished a little wooden chest and an end table."

"In just two weeks?"

"Well, it's pretty quiet in the evenings around there. And Lauren lets me work on them at the gallery when it's not too busy."

Bill nodded thoughtfully. "How about making me your partner on the pie safe?"

"Partner? What do you mean?"

"Well, I just invested twenty dollars. How about I buy the refinishing supplies and we add that to my investment? Then when you sell it, we split the profits according to the amount we put in."

She smiled at his idea, but the temptation to tease him was too hard to resist. "What about all the time and energy I'm going to invest in taking off that old paint?"

He grinned at her. "You really are learning how to dicker."

She laughed, enjoying the moment. "You taught me how."

His smile eased, and a more serious look filled his eyes. "Maybe I could come over and help you with the refinishing."

Her stomach did a funny little dance, and a warm, happy feeling flowed through her. "Sure, that would work. Have you ever done anything like that before?"

"Not really, but I suppose you could teach me."

She sent him a teasing smile. "We'll just add that in as part of my investment."

~

Bill spread out the old blue tarp on the porch floor. A comfortable breeze blew past, cooling his face. Though it was only about seventy-five, he'd worked up a sweat teaming up with Wes to haul the pie safe from the side room of the gallery to the back porch at Long Meadow. The chemicals he and Jenn planned to use to remove the old paint required them to work where there was good ventilation, and this shady area on the north side of the house seemed like the perfect spot.

The screen door opened, and Jenn stepped outside carrying a can of paint remover in one hand and clear plastic bag of supplies in the other. She'd tied her hair up in one of those high, bouncy ponytails that made her look like a teenager. She wore a baggy old yellow shirt he suspected belonged to Wes along with a well-worn pair of jeans with some paint splotches on one knee. But she'd never looked prettier.

He groaned inwardly and told himself to keep his mind on the project. But then she smiled up at him with sparkling green eyes, and he knew it was a lost cause.

"Ready to get to work?" she asked.

He cleared his throat. "Sounds good to me." He pointed to the bag in her hand. "What do you have in there?"

"Everything we need." She pulled out two large pieces of steel wool, a couple paintbrushes, gloves, and some old rags. Then she explained the steps they would take to remove the old paint.

Bill nodded as he listened, enjoying her animated expression and the way she used her hands as she talked. There was something different about her today. He couldn't quite put his finger on it, but she seemed happier and more relaxed. That lifted a weight of concern from his heart that he hadn't even realized he'd been carrying.

They teased each other as they carefully laid the heavy pie safe on the tarp so they could apply the paint remover to the front.

Bill stopped to take a drink of lemonade from one of the glasses sitting on the porch rail. The cool tartness flooded his mouth and washed down his throat. He took the other glass and offered it to Jenn.

"Thanks." She grinned at him over the rim before she lifted her chin and took a long swallow.

He caught a flash of the twisted scar on the side of her neck and quickly shifted his gaze away. Then he looked back, hoping she hadn't noticed his reaction. But he couldn't help it. Each time he saw her scars and thought of the pain she'd experienced, it yanked his emotions in ways he hadn't expected.

It was odd. He'd been on dozens of search and rescue operations, and he'd treated all kinds of injuries, some very serious. But it was different when it was someone you knew, someone you cared about and wanted to protect.

She touched his arm. "Hey, time to quit daydreaming." Her smile reached out and wrapped around his heart, pulling him to her.

He chuckled and tugged on a strand of hair in her ponytail. "I'm ready. Put me to work."

CHAPTER 14

Jenn glanced around the quiet gallery as cool air from the vent overhead ruffled her hair. She looked down at the wooden tray on the counter. Yesterday she'd painted on a base coat of creamy ivory. This morning she planned to add bright-yellow sunflowers surrounded by blue ribbons. Her paints and brushes lay next to the tray, ready for her to get started, but she couldn't drum up much enthusiasm for the project.

She sighed, and her gaze drifted to the window.

Maybe it was the heat. The paper said it would reach ninety-three this afternoon with unusually high humidity for Vermont. Hopefully, the weather wouldn't put a damper on the town's Fourth of July parade and picnic.

Lauren pushed open the front door and stepped in. "We're about ready to go. Sure you won't change your mind and come with us?"

Jenn hesitated, still battling her decision. "Thanks, but I think I'd rather stay here." That wasn't true, but she'd be miserable wearing long sleeves in this heat, and that was her only option.

"I hate to think of you working here by yourself all day."

Lauren's caring smile softened Jenn's resolve, and for a moment she considered telling her the truth. The sound of a car pulling in the gravel driveway stopped her. She looked past Lauren, out the front door. Bill hopped down from the cab of his truck and headed toward the house.

Her heart clenched. She hadn't expected to see him today.

Lauren glanced over her shoulder. "I better get going. We've got to take Toby over to the Elementary school to meet his Cub Scout troop before the parade starts.

Jenn forced a smile. "Okay. Have a good time."

"Thanks." Lauren sent her a concerned glance then pushed open the screen and crossed the gravel driveway toward the house.

Jenn paced to the front window and peeked out. Her spirit sank as she watched Wes greet Bill at the back door and let him in. Lauren followed Bill inside the house. A few seconds later Bill and Wes emerged, each toting a large ice-chest. Jenn had watched Lauren stock them early that morning with bags of ice, sports drinks, bottled water, and boxes of juice. She'd bought enough to keep Toby's entire Cub Scout troop cool.

Bill and Wes loaded the ice-chests into the back of Bill's truck and then stood by the open tailgate talking for a few more seconds.

Tilley and Lauren came out the back door, chatting as they carried picnic baskets toward Wes's car. Toby shut the door and jumped down the back steps. He was dressed in his blue Cub Scout uniform and carried a small American flag. He dashed over and gave Bill a hug.

Tears misted Jenn's eyes as she watched them load up the car. She turned and walked away from the window, wishing she could erase the happy scene from her memory.

She hated to miss the July fourth celebration, but she couldn't imagine making any other choice. Everyone would guess there was something wrong with her if she wore long sleeves today. But exposing her scars and dealing with all the shocked stares and whispered comments would be too painful.

She'd rather avoid everyone and hide her pain. That's what she'd always done. It was the only way she'd survived her parents' death and the daily ache of her aunt and uncle's cruel indifference.

It didn't matter. She could handle it. She walked to the back window and stared out at the lush green meadow behind the gallery. Birds dipped and swooped over the waving grass. Her vision blurred, and her tears overflowed and ran down her cheeks. Her head throbbed, and her stomach felt as though she might lose what little breakfast she had managed to eat.

The front door of the gallery opened.

She gasped and quickly swiped her hands across her cheeks.

"Jenn?" Bill's voice broke the silence.

She slowly turned and faced him, hoping she would not betray her jumbled emotions.

Concern filled his eyes. "Lauren said you're not coming."

She sniffed and focused on straightening a display of collectable tins. "That's right."

He walked up beside her. "Why not?"

"It's too hot." She stepped behind the counter, putting some distance between her and Bill. He was too persuasive, and she didn't think she had the strength to resist him today.

"The parade doesn't start until eleven. I'm sure we could still find a shady spot with a good view." He leaned on the counter and sent her a teasing smile. "That is unless it takes me too long to convince you to change your mind."

Yearning filled her heart, but she quickly squelched it. "I can't go. I told Lauren I'd keep the gallery open."

He lifted his eyebrows at her feeble excuse. "You know she wants you to come. We all do."

She glanced down at her long-sleeved white shirt and black pants. "I'd cook in this outfit."

"Then go change." He glanced at his watch. "We have time. I'll wait."

She felt her tears building again. "You don't understand."

"Then tell me."

She debated her words for a few seconds. "I don't want people staring at me."

His familiar grin surfaced. "No one will tease you about your lily-white skin. I promise."

She shook her head. "That's not what I mean."

"Then what is it?" A hint of impatience edged his words.

A warning flashed through her. If she kept playing guessing games and pushing him away, he'd eventually believe that's what she wanted, but nothing could be further from the truth. She swallowed. "I have . . . some scars from the fire."

He nodded, his expression calm and unchanged. "That's okay. It doesn't matter to the people who care about you."

She released an exasperated huff. "Right." Fighting to control her surging emotions, she turned away and looked out the back window again. The view of the meadow faded as she recalled the look of shock on Phillip's face the night he'd seen her red, blistered face and arms.

Bill closed the space between them and stood silently behind her. Rather than making her feel awkward, his quiet presence comforted her and infused her with courage.

She fiddled with the bottom hem of her shirt. "I was engaged . . . before I came up here."

He waited a few seconds before he spoke. "What happened?"

She slowly turned and faced him. "Phillip took one look at me after the fire and walked away."

Anger flashed across Bill's face. "Then he was a fool."

"He said he loved me."

"Then he lied."

Confusion and pain flooded her heart. Her throat burned and her eyes stung.

Bill's expression softened as he stepped closer and pulled her in for a hug. "I'm sorry, Jenn. That didn't come out right." He held her a moment more, then stepped back. "Maybe he just didn't know what love is."

She sniffed and grabbed a tissue from under the counter. "I don't know why I'm crying about this. It's been almost four months. I should be over it by now."

"Four months isn't such a long time if you really loved him."

She wiped her nose as she considered Bill's words. She thought she loved Phillip, but she wasn't so sure now. If she was honest, the pain of his rejection hurt more than the loss of his love. She pushed that thought away, uncertain if her stormy emotions were playing tricks on her.

"I don't blame Phillip. I looked awful. My face was swollen and ugly, and the burns on my arm and neck looked even worse than they do now."

The muscles in Bill's jaw flickered, but he didn't look away.

"He wasn't the only one who couldn't deal with it. Most of my friends were afraid to visit me in the hospital, and when I got out, they had all kinds of excuses for not seeing me."

"Then you need new friends," he said gently, "people who really care about you."

A powerful longing rose in her heart. Were there really people who wouldn't be repulsed by her scars, who would love and accept her in spite of them?

He reached for her hand. "Jenn, listen to me. Not everyone who sees your burns is going to turn their back and walk away." He waited a moment, as though he wanted those words to sink in. "Trust me, Jenn. Show me."

She glanced down at his warm, strong hand holding hers. Comfort and assurance flowed from his grasp. The invitation was risky, but if she could show Bill, maybe she would have the courage to show others.

She slipped her hand out of his and unbuttoned her right cuff with shaky fingers. Her heart pounded loudly in her ears. She slowly rolled up her sleeve and turned over her arm, exposing the red twisted scar that traveled up past her elbow and disappeared into her sleeve. "It goes all the way up." She looked at him, dreading his response.

He reached over and lightly traced the edge of her scar with his finger. "Does it still hurt?"

She swallowed and struggled to find her voice. "Not so much now. My shoulder is still sore. The burns were deeper there."

He nodded, his gaze traveling over the arm, taking in the details.

"It looks awful, doesn't it?" She bit her lip, hoping he'd disagree, but knowing that would be a lie.

"The only thing that bothers me is thinking how much this must have hurt you."

His caring words poured over her heart like a healing balm. She lifted her gaze to meet his.

"I mean it, Jenn. It doesn't matter to me."

"Thank you," she whispered.

Warmth and affection filled his eyes as his gaze traveled over her face and hair. She held her breath, waiting, wondering if he would lean closer and kiss her.

But instead, he sent her a tender smile. Then he glanced at his watch. "We still have time to catch the parade if you want, or we can go over to the Park and meet everyone there."

Jenn swallowed, feeling like she was trying to regain her balance after being on an amusement park ride.

She looked down at her arm and studied her scars. Showing Bill was one thing. He was kind and caring, but what about other people? What would happen when everyone else saw them?

"Hey, it'll be okay." He gently ran his finger down the side of her cheek.

Fighting the voice that told her she was a fool to listen to him, she leaned into his touch and looked up into his eyes once more.

"I'll be right there with you," he said. "I promise."

The sweetness of those words warmed her heart, sealing her decision. "Okay. I'll go change." She smiled at him once more and hurried off to the house.

CHAPTER 15

*J*enn leaned back and looked up through the lacy branches overhead. The silver birch leaves flickered in the wind, revealing patches of azure sky and sending shifting patterns of sunlight over her face.

Closing her eyes, she felt the breeze on her neck and arms and released a deep sigh. This was bliss. The weather had changed, bringing cooler temperatures and blowing away much of the uncomfortable humidity.

They'd finished a delicious picnic supper a few minutes earlier. Jenn had enjoyed the barbecued chicken, oriental coleslaw, fruit salad, Tilley's homemade rolls, and Bill's special fudge brownies.

While they ate, Tilley shared memories of celebrating the Fourth of July with her family on the coast of Maine when she was young. Toby entertained them with some silly jokes he had learned from his friends at school. And Bill told several crazy stories about his college days when he and Wes were roommates. Wes denied them, but Bill insisted most of the stories were true. Lauren and Jenn laughed so hard they begged Bill to stop and give them a break. Jenn couldn't remember when she'd enjoyed a day more, and she tucked away all those happy moments in her heart.

Lifting her hand, she shaded her eyes and searched the park. She spotted Bill, Wes, and Toby just past the gazebo, lined up to take part in the watermelon seed-spitting contest. Tilley sat nearby in a lawn chair, chatting with an older man who held tightly to his dog's leash while his excited Boston bull terrier pulled to keep moving.

Lauren kneeled beside her on the picnic blanket, cleaning up the remains of their meal. She snapped the lid on the brownie container and placed it in the basket. "You look great in that outfit."

Jenn smiled. "Thanks, but I still feel bad about borrowing it without asking."

"Stop apologizing. I'm glad you did. I hope you'll keep it."

"Oh, I couldn't do that."

"Please?" Lauren wiggled her eyebrows and grinned. "Then I can put a new shorts outfit on my honeymoon shopping list."

Jenn chuckled. "Okay. If you put it that way, I guess I could keep them." She loved the cute denim shorts and red t-shirt with the American flag on the front. Wearing them made her feel cool and comfortable, and so far no one had said anything about her scars.

She gazed across the park at Bill. He was probably right. It didn't bother Wes and Lauren, and Tilley was so sweet she'd never say anything unkind.

Toby raced across the grass toward them. "Bill spit farther than anybody!" He plopped down on the blanket beside his mother. His face was red and sweaty from his time in the sun. Watermelon juice stained his mouth and ran down his chin.

"Come here, sweetie." Lauren reached into the picnic basket and pulled out a container of wipes.

Toby leaned forward, squeezed his eyes shut, and pressed his lips together tightly, while Lauren wiped his cheeks and chin.

"Are your hands sticky?" she asked, and he held them out for her to inspect.

Bill strode toward them and took a seat on the blanket next to Jenn.

She glanced over at him and laughed when she saw juice and seeds running down his arms and dripping off his elbows. "Wow, you really got into that contest."

He grinned, a triumphant look in his blue eyes. "I may be a mess, but I won."

Wes sat down beside Lauren. "Man, pass me those wipes when you're done, honey."

Lauren was still helping Toby. So Jenn reached over, pulled out two wipes, and held them out to Wes.

Toby gasped and shrunk back toward Lauren. His mouth twisted into a painful grimace as he stared at Jenn's arm. "What happened to you?"

Jenn dropped the wipes and pulled her arm back to her chest.

"Toby, hush!" Lauren turned to Jenn, distress clouding her eyes. "I'm sorry."

A hopeless weight descended on Jenn's heart. What could she say? She was sorry, too. Sorry she'd worn this t-shirt and frightened her nephew.

"It's okay, Toby." Bill picked up the wipes and began cleaning his hands. "Your Aunty Jenn has some scars from getting burned, but they don't hurt her anymore."

Confusion filled Toby's eyes as he shifted his gaze to Bill.

Bill scooted over next to Toby. "It's no big deal. Lots of people have scars." His matter-of-fact tone eased some of the tension. "I've got one right here on my hand."

Toby leaned closer to look. "How'd you get that?"

"When I went camping last summer, I grabbed hold of a hot pan without thinking, and I got burned."

Toby examined the small red scar on Bill's right hand then looked up. "Did it hurt?"

"You better believe it!" Bill shook his hand and made a painful face. "Yowie!"

Toby giggled.

"Hey, what are you laughing at?" Bill poked him in the ribs with a teasing grin. "You should've seen me. I dropped that pan faster than you can say, 'Yes, ma'am!' Then I jumped around the fire, waving my hand in the air and shouting until I came to my senses. Finally, I ran down to the lake and stuck my hand in the cold water." He made a hissing sound like steam rising from the water. "Ahh, that made it feel better."

Toby laughed so hard he doubled over and grabbed his stomach.

Jenn felt her own laughter bubble to the surface, and gratitude flooded her heart. Bill had used his gift of humor to shift the focus away from her and lighten the moment.

"How about you, Toby?" Bill asked. "Do you have any scars?"

The little boy sobered and looked at his mom. "Do I?"

She nodded. "Check your right knee."

He pulled his knee up for a closer look.

Lauren pointed to a faint line about an inch long, running down one side of his kneecap. "When you were three you fell off the slide at the park. The cut healed in a week or so, but you still have that little scar to remind you to be careful." She smiled at him and ruffled his blond hair off his forehead.

Toby bit his lip then turned to Wes. "Do you have any scars?"

"I sure do. Right here." Wes pointed to his left side of his face where a faint, jagged line ran along his cheekbone.

Toby lifted his finger and traced the scar, a frown creasing his forehead. "How'd that happen?"

"I got it from some men who didn't like me telling people about Jesus."

Toby nodded, his face solemn. "My mom told me about that. They put you in jail and were real mean to you, but you were brave."

Wes laid his hand on Toby's shoulder. "Well, God helped me get out of there, and then He brought me here to Vermont to meet you and your mom." He shifted his gaze to Lauren.

"And your scar is better now?" Toby asked.

"That's right," Wes said. "God designed our bodies to heal themselves. Sometimes He uses doctors and medicine to help us get well, but usually we just need to rest and take care of ourselves, and we get better." He smiled at Toby. "That's a pretty good plan, don't you think?"

Toby nodded, a serious, thoughtful expression on his face. He shifted his gaze to Jenn. "I'm sorry you got burned," he said softly. "But I'm glad God's healing you."

Jenn's throat tightened, and she had to force out her words. "Thanks, Toby."

He smiled at her, his blue eyes shining. He obviously had no problem believing God could heal any pain or fix any problem.

If only she could believe as easily as Toby.

Lauren beamed at her son. "Come here, big guy. We need to finish getting you cleaned up."

Bill stood and looked down at Jenn. "You want to go for a walk?"

"Sure." She stood, thankful he seemed to sense she could use a break and some time to settle her emotions.

They strolled past several groups of people sitting on picnic blankets and lawn chairs. Children ran by, laughing and chasing each other. A mother called her toddler back to her side.

They passed the gazebo where musicians were tuning their instruments in preparation for the band concert due to begin at sunset. The chorus of insects grew louder as they reached the path that circled the lake.

"Are you okay?" he asked, breaking the comfortable silence between them.

"Yes, thanks to you." Their arms brushed, and awareness flowed through Jenn. "I didn't know what to say to Toby, but you handled it perfectly."

He tucked his hands in his pockets, looking a little embarrassed. "Ah, I was just goofing around with him."

"It was more than that. You helped him understand, and that was really . . . great." She wished she could explain how much his kindness and sensitivity meant to her. No one else had stepped in to help her like that in a very long time.

Bill's gaze drifted off toward the lake. "I guess it's natural for kids to be curious."

"I suppose so." She bent and plucked a flower that looked like a yellow daisy.

"Coreopsis."

"What?"

"That's a coreopsis." He pointed to the flower in her hand.

"Oh, thanks." She smiled. "I didn't know the name."

"Well, you do now." He grinned back at her.

She twirled the flower in her fingers as they walked on. Her feeling of connection with Bill had deepened today.

The sun dipped lower over the lake, and the sky took on an orange and golden glow in the west. The breeze blowing off the lake sent a little shiver through her, and she wrapped her arms around herself.

"Are you cold?"

"Just a little." For a second she thought he might slip his arm around her, but instead he gestured toward the parking lot.

"Let's walk back to the truck. I've got an extra sweatshirt in there."

Disappointment tugged at her heart, but she chased it away, telling herself she was being silly. Bill was a caring friend. That's all. But she couldn't help wishing he wanted to be more than that.

∽

An hour later they sat side-by-side on the picnic blanket listening to the band play Broadway show tunes and patriotic songs. Bill stole a glance at Jenn and smiled. She looked cute in his big sweatshirt with the cuffs rolled up and her knees tucked up to her chest. He leaned a little closer, telling himself he was trying to block the breeze from the lake and keep her warm, but the truth was, he just enjoyed being near her.

Darkness settled over the park. A hum of excitement ran through the crowd as the band played the final song.

"Do you think they'll make it back in time?" Jenn scanned the crowd, searching for Wes, Lauren, and Toby.

"I'm not sure. The lines for the port-a-potties could be long." He chuckled. "That's just like Toby, deciding he has to go right when the fireworks are going to start."

"I guess it might take them a while to go back to the car and get Lauren's sweater, too."

Bill nodded, but he didn't mind. Tilley had gone to sit with friends from church, leaving Jenn and Bill alone to enjoy the music. And though the park was full of people, there was only one person occupying his thoughts.

The music rose to a crescendo, and the first fireworks whistled into the sky and exploded. The ground shook, and a dazzling cloud of red, white, and blue stars burst overhead.

Jenn pulled in a sharp breath. The crowd cheered and clapped as the sparkling trails rained down, fading into the night sky. A few embers still glowed as they dropped into the dark waters of the lake.

They were only about fifty yards from the fireworks setup and heard the whooshing sound as the next shells blasted off. Jenn tensed and leaned closer to Bill. The shells exploded into a fiery cluster of golden stars.

He laid his hand on her shoulder. "It's pretty loud. Are you okay?"

She nodded, but when three more shells exploded in quick succession, she covered her ears and turned her face into his shoulder.

Frustration rolled through him. She had a good reason to hate the loud blasts. He made a quick decision and tugged her to her feet. "Come on. Let's go."

Jenn blinked at him. "Where are we going?"

"Trust me." He led her through the crowd, holding her hand. Each time another shell burst, she tightened her grip and picked up her pace, confirming his decision.

When they reached his truck, he unlocked the passenger door for her, and she hopped in.

He hustled around and climbed in his side, quickly shutting the door and blocking out most of the sound.

She sent him a worried glance. "I'm sorry. We don't have to leave."

"We're not." He inserted his key in the ignition, took a CD from the holder on his visor, and slid it into the CD player. "Go ahead. Adjust the volume. You can play it as loud as you want."

She glanced out through the windshield where they had a perfect view of the fireworks, and understanding glowed in her eyes. "This is great. Thank you."

He grinned. "You're welcome."

She set the volume loud enough to cover some of the noise from the explosions, but not so loud that they couldn't still carry on a conversation. Then she smiled and settled back, looking blissfully happy.

He scooted closer and slipped his arm across the back of

the seat. He played with a strand of her hair for a few minutes and finally rested his arm around her shoulder. She leaned closer, and he caught the scent of flowers in her hair. He couldn't have orchestrated a better ending to the evening, sitting next to her and watching the delight on her face as the fireworks burst into dazzling colors against the night sky.

They watched for about ten more minutes. The CD paused between songs just as the grand finale began. The sound of the multiple explosions filled the air, and even inside the truck they felt the vibrations.

Jenn tensed, but didn't hide her face this time. Instead, she lifted her gaze to the sky as round after round exploded in glittering bursts of color. "Oh, it's so beautiful."

His throat tightened as he watched her smile spread wider and saw the sparkling fireworks reflected in her eyes. "Yes," he murmured, "beautiful."

When the last firework drifted down, she sighed and settled back. "That was amazing." Turning to him, she sent him a sweet smile. "Thanks, Bill."

"So, you liked watching it from in here?"

"Yes, this was a great idea."

"I'm glad you decided to come."

"I'm glad you made me."

He pulled back and laughed. "Made you?"

"Well, convinced me." The teasing light in her eyes sent his pulse racing, but he suspected she had no idea what she did to his heart.

He settled his arm around her shoulder again and ran his fingers through her silky hair. The intoxicating warmth of her nearness filled him with a longing to tell her how beautiful she was to him.

But he sensed a warning. He and Jenn didn't share a spiritual connection. They could never build a lasting relationship without that, at least he couldn't. He shifted his gaze away, trying to focus and straighten out his tangled thoughts.

"What is it?" she asked, her voice soft as a caress.

He turned back to her. She watched him with luminous eyes, reflecting a sweet openness he'd longed to see there since the first day they met. The warning faded, and he could no longer remember why he shouldn't tell her everything in his heart. He leaned closer and gently ran his finger down the side of her face. "Today was great."

She looked up at him with a shy smile. "I had a good time, too."

He swallowed and wished for the millionth time that he was better at putting his thoughts and feelings into words. "Can I tell you something?"

"Sure."

"Since you moved over to Lauren's, I've realized—"

A loud knock on the passenger window startled them. Bill shifted his gaze as Jenn pulled back and turned toward the sound.

Wes stood outside the truck, a frustrated expression on his face as he signaled for them to roll down the window.

Jenn leaned over and pushed the button. "Hey, Wes."

"Man, I've been looking all over for you guys. I was worried. I didn't know what happened to you."

Bill leaned toward Wes. "We decided to watch the fireworks from in here."

Wes studied them with a concerned look. "Well next time you want to take off like that, it would be nice to let someone know."

"Sorry, Wes." Jenn pressed her lips together and slid a few more inches away from Bill. "It was pretty loud down there by the lake, so Bill brought me up here."

Wes rubbed the back of his neck and looked like there was a lot more he'd like to say. He shifted his gaze to Jenn. "Are you ready to head back to Lauren's?"

She glanced over her shoulder at Bill, uncertainty in her eyes.

"You've got a full car. I'll take her home." Bill turned the key in the ignition. Before Wes could protest, the truck rumbled to life. He clamped his jaw tightly and tried to ignore the perturbed glance Wes shot over his shoulder as he walked away.

CHAPTER 16

*B*ill pulled into the parking lot at the nature center, grabbed his Styrofoam carryout container from the Green Mountain Cafe, and climbed out of the truck. He spotted Wes's car still parked in the corner under the trees. They usually had lunch together, but not yesterday or today.

Since the Fourth of July an uncomfortable tension seemed to stretch between them. Bill had left for work early without seeing Wes at home. Wes brought his lunch both days, making Bill suspect he'd planned that so they wouldn't have to go out to lunch together.

Bill pushed open the door and stepped into the hallway leading to his office. Avoiding each other like this was crazy. They'd been good friends for over nine years and gone through too much to let a little misunderstanding pull them apart. But for some reason Bill didn't want to be the first one to bring it up.

There was no reason for Wes to be mad at him. He and Jenn hadn't done anything wrong. But the strained silence was getting to him. Maybe it was time to sit down and talk things over with Wes.

Bill opened his office door and scanned the empty room.

No sign of Wes or anyone else. Lowering himself into his desk chair, he opened the takeout box. The aroma of the hot corned beef, sauerkraut, and Swiss cheese made his mouth water.

As he lifted the warm Reuben sandwich and took a bite, his office door flew open. Matt Jacobson, one of his summer interns, poked his head in. "You're not going to believe this."

Bill quickly swallowed a mouthful of corned beef. "What?"

"Come on out front. You'll see." Matt grinned and disappeared out the door.

Bill got up and followed him to the front porch. Wes and two other interns, Mandy and Troy, stood in a circle peering into a cardboard box. Matt joined them.

Bill crossed the porch. "What is it?"

Wes stood back, making room for Bill. "Take a look."

Bill glanced into the box. Three small tan puppies slept in a pile surrounded by an old brown blanket. "Wow, where'd they come from?" Bill knelt down to take a closer look.

Wes squatted next to him. "We don't know. I just found them out here a few minutes ago."

Bill ran his hand over the head of one of the sleepy puppies. "Look like Golden retrievers or Labradors. Probably mixed. I don't think they would've been abandoned if they were purebred."

Troy frowned. "So, why'd somebody leave them here?"

"I guess they know we love animals, and they're hoping we'll find homes for them," Wes said.

Bill rubbed his chin. How was he going to manage that?

"My brother might take one." Matt slipped his hands in his pants pockets. "They lost a dog about three months ago, and they're talking about getting another one. I could give him a call."

Bill nodded. "That would be great, Matt."

"I'd love to have one." Mandy leaned down and picked

up the smallest puppy. "I don't know if my landlord will let me have a dog, but I can ask."

The little puppy yawned and snuggled into Mandy's neck. Bill chuckled. They'd make great pets for someone who had the time and patience to care for them. Surely, there was someone who needed the love and companionship a dog could bring.

An idea popped into his head, and his smile spread wider. Maybe he could find an owner for the third puppy without too much trouble at all.

∽

Jenn clipped off a wilted geranium bloom and dropped it into the bucket at her feet. She slowly twirled the pot to be sure she'd found all the dried blossoms, then hung it back up on the hook above the porch rail. Sunshine sparkled through the tall trees, and a gentle breeze lifted the hair off her neck. She took down the next pot and checked the flowers.

Business had been slow in the gallery this afternoon, so she had volunteered to work outdoors. She'd spent the last hour weeding and watering the flowerbeds around Tilley's back porch. It felt good, working with the sun on her back and the warm dirt in her hands. Jenn glanced down at the neat, weed-free flowerbeds and smiled. Bright marigolds and petunias surrounded the roses and white hydrangeas. Tilley would be pleased.

A warm sense of contentment filled her as she dumped the clippings on the compost pile and walked over to turn on the hose. She rinsed her hands, enjoying the feeling of the warm water changing to cool as it poured over her fingers. Leaning down, she slurped a quick drink and then pulled the hose over to water the hanging pots.

A black truck pulled into the long drive. Recognition zinged along Jenn's nerves, and her heartbeat quickened. She hadn't seen Bill for two days, since they'd been together on the Fourth of July, but he'd never been far from her thoughts. The memory of watching the fireworks with him in the privacy of his truck replayed through her mind and warmed her cheeks. She wasn't sure what he might have said if her brother hadn't interrupted them, but guessing sent her heart on a wild ride.

The truck rolled to a stop, and Bill climbed out. He looked tan and handsome in a light blue knit shirt with Wild River Nature Center stitched above the pocket. She pulled in a calming breath and waved to him.

Bill grinned and closed his door. "You look like you're working hard."

"I am." She returned his smile, shut off the hose, and walked over to meet him. "So, what brings you out our way?"

His eyes glowed as he smiled at her. "I've got something to show you." He walked around to the passenger side of the truck and opened the door.

Jenn followed him, curiosity prickling through her. "What is it?"

"Take a look." Bill lifted out a medium-sized cardboard box and lowered it to the ground at her feet.

She leaned over the box and gasped. A darling little puppy with sandy-gold hair cocked his head and looked up at her. "Oh, my goodness. Look at him! He's beautiful."

"Well, he is a she." Bill chuckled. "But you're right. She's pretty."

"Can I pick her up?"

"Sure." He stuffed his hands in his jeans pockets, watching her with a pleased smile.

Jenn lifted the puppy out of the box and cradled her in her arms. She was soft and warm and full of life. Memories of Beau flooded back as the puppy wiggled up close and licked Jenn's cheek. "She's adorable."

"Let's take her over on the grass so she can explore a little."

Out front, tall maple trees shaded the lush green lawn. Jenn set the puppy down and watched her sniff the grass. "Where'd you get her?"

A frown creased Bill's forehead. "Someone abandoned her and two other puppies at the nature center."

"They just dropped them off?"

"Yeah. We found them on the front porch this afternoon."

Jenn watched the puppy bite a small stick and drag it a few feet across the grass. "So, are you going to keep her?" she asked, her voice soft and wistful.

Bill rubbed his chin. "Well, I know how much you miss Beau, so I thought you might like to have her."

Jenn gasped. "Really? Oh, Bill." She reached for him and gave him a hug. His arms encircled her, pulling her closer. She nestled against his chest and closed her eyes as a thousand happy thoughts danced through her heart.

But a question rose and tempered her joy. She stepped back and looked up at him. "I wonder if Tilley and Lauren will mind?" She glanced at the puppy again, longing growing in her heart.

Bill tenderly tucked a strand of hair behind her ear. "I already talked to Tilley. I didn't want to bring the puppy over and get your hopes up if she wasn't open to it."

Jenn's eyes widened. "She said yes?"

Grinning, he nodded.

She squealed and hugged him again, wishing she could explain how much this meant. Maybe there was a way she could show him. Pushing away her doubts, she stood on tiptoe and kissed his cheek. "Thank you, Bill. This is just the best—"

The screen door squeaked open behind her. Bill looked up, and Jenn felt him tense. She turned and saw her brother standing on the porch. Questions clouded his eyes as he surveyed them.

Bill dropped his arms and took a step back. His expression sobered as he met Wes's gaze.

Apprehension rippled through Jenn as she looked first at Wes and then Bill.

"Dinner's ready." Wes let the screen door close behind him.

"Look at the puppy Bill brought me." Jenn bent down and picked her up. "Isn't she sweet?"

Wes's expression eased as he shifted his gaze to the dog. "Yeah, she's real nice." But his smile didn't reach his eyes.

"It's okay," Jenn said. "Bill already talked to Tilley. She said I could keep her." She waited, hoping Wes would say something to explain his sober mood, but he turned and walked back inside.

When the screen door banged closed, she turned to Bill. "What's the matter with Wes?"

Bill squinted toward the door. "I'm not sure." But the troubled look in his eyes made her wonder if he knew more than he was saying.

∼

BILL SAT on his bed and flipped on his laptop. Maybe he would catch up on email or work on his Bible study. He wasn't in the mood to talk to Wes tonight. That's why he'd headed into his room as soon as he heard Wes's car pull in the driveway a few minutes earlier.

A knock sounded at his bedroom door. Before Bill could answer, the door opened.

"Got a minute?" A muscle flicked in Wes's jaw as he waited for Bill's answer.

"Sure. Come on in." Bill closed his laptop and braced himself for the conflict that seemed to be brewing.

Wes stepped in and faced him. "I need to know what's going on with you and Jenn."

Bill's shoulders tensed. "What do you mean?"

"I mean . . . seeing you two together in your truck the night of the fourth and then today at Lauren's makes it look like things have moved way past friendship."

Bill huffed and set his computer aside.

Wes walked over and stood at the end of the bed. "You may think I'm out of line, but I don't want her to get hurt."

"I'd never hurt Jenn. You know me better than that."

"I thought I did, but I'm not so sure now."

"Hey, you're the one who said we need to take care of her, spend time with her, win her over. That was our plan."

"So that's what you're doing?" Wes's question cut straight to Bill's heart.

"Well, that's the way it started. Now, I'm not so sure."

"Man, I should've considered where this could go when I convinced you to let her stay here."

"Yeah, well I guess neither one of us thought that through very well." Bill sank back on his pillows with a heavy sigh.

"Did you know she was engaged before she came up here?"

"Yeah, she told me." Bill narrowed his eye. "It's a good thing that jerk lives on the other side of the country."

Wes frowned. "What do you mean?"

Why hadn't Jenn told her brother how Phillip had treated her? "He came to the hospital the night of the fire, but when he saw her burns, he walked out on her, and she hasn't seen him since."

Wes sighed rubbed his eyes. "No wonder she doesn't want to talk about it."

Bill nodded, wishing there was something he could do to make up for all those painful experiences. It didn't seem right that one person had to deal with so many losses and betrayals.

Wes sat on the end of the bed. "Look, I understand why you're attracted to Jenn. She's really special. But she's not committed to the Lord, and you know what the Bible says about being unequally yoked."

"Yeah, I know." Bill's stomach ached like he'd swallowed a heavy rock. "I've been praying for her and looking for a chance to talk to her about it."

"And?" A hopeful light flickered in Wes's eyes.

"So far it hasn't happened." Bill clenched his jaw and stared at the ceiling. How had things gotten so mixed up? He'd started out with good intention and pure motives. He was going to help her rediscover her faith and overcome the pain of her past. But somewhere along the line, his growing feelings had sent him down a selfish path, pursuing Jenn without really thinking about what was right or best for her.

He laid his arm over his eyes. "I can't believe it. She's been here almost six weeks, and I have no idea if she's one inch closer to the Lord."

Wes scooted back and leaned against the wall. "Lauren said she's had some good conversations with her. She gave her a Bible the other night." Wes squinted toward the window, pain etched on his face. "But Jenn blames God for our parents' death."

"Yeah, she told me the same thing, said she prayed her heart out, but they died anyway. She thinks that proves God doesn't care about her or answer prayer." It hurt Bill to repeat it, but it was important for Wes to understand. How else could he help his sister?

Wes sighed. "There's got to be some way to get through to her."

How could they help Jenn see the truth? Bill's mind went blank as he searched for an answer. What if she never made a commitment to the Lord? What would happen then? That thought squeezed the air from his chest. He fought it off and pulled in a deep breath. "She'll come around. I know she will."

"Well . . . until she does, you need to back off."

Bill stiffened. "What?"

"You're going to break her heart if you keep leading her on. That could push her farther away from God and close the door for good."

Heat flashed up his neck and into his face. "I'm not leading her on. I care about her."

"I know you do . . . but you've got to wait. Give God time to work without the distractions of a relationship getting in the way."

Bill sat up, a debate raging in his heart. "It'll hurt her more if I just drop out of her life. She's not going to understand."

"You don't have to ignore her, just stop pursuing her. Take a step back, treat her like a sister."

Bill grimaced. How was he going to do that? Every time she was near he felt like some huge magnet drew them together. It wouldn't work. He'd have to leave the state if he was going to stay away from Jennifer Evans.

Wes clamped his hand on Bill's shoulder. "I know this is hard. But you've got to think of what's best for Jenn."

Everything in him told him Wes was wrong. He had to be. Jenn needed him.

But a quiet voice confirmed the truth. *Let her go. Trust me. That's what love would do.*

CHAPTER 17

Jenn slipped the periwinkle-blue bridesmaid dress over her head and let it slide down past her shoulders. The satin felt smooth and cool against her skin. She adjusted the straps and turned to face the fitting room mirror.

Her eyes widened, and a small gasp escaped her mouth. The dress looked beautiful, more beautiful than any costume she'd worn on stage at the dinner theater. The beaded bodice and A-line style accentuated her slim figure and made her feel feminine and elegant.

Her smile faded as her gaze moved to her right arm and shoulder where the mottled and twisted scars spread across her exposed skin.

The scene at the Fourth of July picnic replayed through her mind, tightening her stomach into a hard knot. One glance at her scars and Toby had drawn back in horror. And what he'd seen was nothing compared to the scars on her shoulder where doctors had used a skin graft to repair the third-degree burns.

She forced her gaze away and reached behind her for the

zipper. After pulling it up only a few inches, pain shot through her shoulder. She dropped her hands in defeat.

"How does it look?" Julia called from the other side of the curtain. "Can I come in?"

Jenn gasped. "Just a minute." She grabbed the matching jacket and slipped it on. The translucent organza wouldn't completely hide her burns, but at least they would be a little less noticeable. She tugged on the three-quarter-length sleeves, pulling them down as far as possible. Then she checked the mirror one last time. "Okay, you can come in."

Julia pulled back the curtain. "Oh, wow, you look great! That color's perfect for you." She stepped inside the fitting room and let the curtain fall back.

Jenn stared at Julia, and her stomach tumbled. She looked stunning in the strapless dress, minus the jacket. Her smooth, golden-tanned skin glowed against the bright blue fabric, and her shapely figure filled out the dress in ways Jenn never could. A little vine of envy wrapped around her heart, squeezing out all the joy she'd felt moments before.

"Turn around." Julia's blue eyes sparkled, their color perfectly matching the shade of the dress. "Let's see how it looks in the back."

Heat burned Jenn's face as she rotated under Julia's inspection.

"Oh, let me help you with the zipper."

Jenn froze, and a queasy lightheaded feeling washed over her. She didn't want to take off the jacket and show anyone her scars, especially perfect Julia, but there was no way around it. They couldn't do a final fitting without zipping the dress up all the way. Keeping her back to Julia, she slid the jacket off and laid it on the bench.

Julia zipped her up. "There. Let's see how it looks now."

Jenn slowly turned around, steeling herself for Julia's reaction.

Julia's gaze traveled over her, flickering for just an instant at shoulder level, but her smile never faltered. "It's perfect. You look beautiful."

Confusion swirled through Jenn, and she ducked her chin. How could Julia say that? Didn't she see the way her ugly scars screamed for attention?

Julia stepped closer and touched Jenn's arm. "I mean it, Jenn. You look lovely." Her voice grew softer. "Don't worry about your shoulder. No one will even notice."

"But it looks awful." Tears flooded Jenn's eyes. "I don't even like to look at it."

Julia took her hand. "Hey, beauty is more than perfect skin, or shiny hair, or a great figure. It comes from who you are inside, in your heart. It shines out through your eyes and your smile. And that's what touches people and draws them to you." Julia squeezed her hand gently then let it go.

"I don't feel very beautiful on the inside either." Jenn's voice came out like a cracked whisper. She reached up and brushed a tear from her cheek, feeling like a fool for crying. Now Julia would know her scars weren't just on her arm and shoulder, they were burned deep in her heart and mind, telling her she could never be beautiful again.

Julia's eyes shone and a soft smile played on her lips. "God loves you, Jenn. He wants to give you that kind of beauty that never fades or changes. It comes from a heart surrendered to Him."

A familiar longing stirred inside Jenn. She tried to grab hold of what Julia meant, but she felt like it slipped away. "I don't understand."

"You will." Julia looked in the mirror with her. "He's already working in there." She gently tapped the area over Jenn's heart. "I can tell."

Julia's words warmed her, like a tiny flame of hope catching fire and burning brighter. Could it be true? Did God still care about her even though she'd turned away and refused to acknowledge him for almost ten years? Before she could form an answer, doubts rose and quenched the flame. "I don't see much evidence of God working in my life."

"Well, I do. He brought you here to Vermont. He gave you a job at the gallery. You're here to share Wes and Lauren's special day. And that's just the beginning."

Jenn pressed her lips together and looked away from their reflection. Julia seemed to think God was behind everything that happened in life. But she'd only mentioned the good things. What about all the painful, difficult experiences Jenn had gone through? How would Julia explain those? Was God behind them, too?

"I'll be right back." Julia pushed aside the curtain and stepped out.

Jenn sat on the bench, her thoughts drifting back to her conversation with Lauren a few weeks ago. She'd said God could bring good out of even the worst times. Maybe Jenn should ask her more about that. Perhaps Lauren could help her sort out these painful questions and figure out how to reconnect with God.

Julia returned wearing her organza jacket. "Why don't we both wear the jacket for the ceremony, then, when it's time for the reception, you can decide if we take them off or not. Either way is okay with me."

Jenn stood. "You don't have to do that. You look great without it."

"It's more important to me that you feel comfortable and enjoy your brother's wedding."

Jenn blew out a deep breath. "Okay, thanks." How could she have been envious of Julia? She was sweet and caring, and she obviously wanted to be her friend.

"How's it going in there?" Lauren called. "Ready to show me your dresses?"

Jenn nodded to Julia. She pulled back the curtain, and they stepped out.

Lauren stood in front of them wearing her shimmering

white wedding gown with a softly scalloped sweetheart neckline, beaded straps and bodice, and a flowing A-line skirt. More beading swirled along the hem.

Jenn's breath caught in her throat. "Oh . . . wow, you look amazing!"

Julia grabbed Lauren's hands. "Wait until Wes sees you. You're going to knock him right off his feet!"

Lauren laughed, and her cheeks glowed pink behind her cinnamon-tinted freckles. "You really think he'll like it?" She picked up the skirt and turned so they could see the back. "Look at the train." She smiled as she looked over her shoulder.

"It's beautiful." Julia straightened Lauren's veil. "You look like a princess."

"Thanks." Lauren floated around and faced them again. "How do you like your dresses? Do they fit okay?"

Jenn ran her hand over the smooth satin fabric. "I love the color, and the jacket is perfect."

"You both look great."

For the next few minutes, the girls laughed and talked as they took turns standing on a raised platform. The woman who did the alterations checked each dress one last time for any final adjustments.

When it was Julia's turn, she smiled into the mirror catching Lauren's reflection. "I can't wait to see Wes and Bill in their tuxes. Did you decide on the blue cummerbunds or the black?"

Jenn's ears perked up at the mention of Bill's name. She hadn't seen him since the day he'd brought her the puppy. He hadn't called either, not even to check and see how little Sophie was doing.

She didn't understand it. He'd been so wonderful on the Fourth, and then, two days later, he seemed happy to see her and eager to give her the puppy.

Had she said or done something that pushed him away?

Maybe she shouldn't have hugged him. But he hadn't seemed upset about it. In fact, he'd welcomed her into his arms.

So, if the hug wasn't the problem, then it had to be the kiss on the cheek. She should've known that would make him uncomfortable. He obviously didn't want more than friendship, and that little peck must have crossed some invisible line and sent up a red flag for him.

What did she expect? He'd made his feelings clear. And how many times had she told herself the same thing—she didn't want a romantic relationship right now. Her life was too unsettled . . . but lately her heart had been tugging her in a different direction. Could he have sensed her growing feelings? Was that the problem?

"Jenn?"

She blinked and looked up at Lauren. "Sorry, I missed what you said."

"It's almost four. We better change. There's still a lot to do to get ready for Tilley's party."

"Oh. Right." Jenn took one last glance in the mirror. It didn't matter how pretty she looked in this dress, with or without the jacket. The only person she wanted to impress wasn't going to give her a second look.

CHAPTER 18

Bill stepped up on the porch at Long Meadow and knocked at the back door. Clutching a gift bag in one hand, he looked through the screen, but he didn't see anyone in the mudroom or kitchen.

Tilley had told him he didn't need to knock, but the prospect of running into Jenn unannounced made his palms sweat and his heart bang out a wild rhythm.

Maybe he ought to just leave Tilley's birthday gift on the kitchen counter and hightail it back to his truck. He huffed out a disgusted breath. He was not going to let his misguided feelings for Jenn ruin his friendships with everyone else.

Lately he'd felt like a lonely outcast as he tried to avoid Jenn, which also meant staying away from Tilley, Lauren, Toby and most of the time, even Wes.

When Lauren called yesterday and invited him over for Tilley's birthday dinner, he told her he'd stop by after dinner to bring Tilley a present. Spending the whole evening with Jenn would be too difficult, but he couldn't resist seeing them all for a little while.

He pushed open the screen door and stepped inside. "Anybody home?" The little puppy he had given Jenn raised her head and trotted across the mudroom toward him. He knelt and scratched behind her ears. "Hey there. How you doing?" The puppy wiggled with delight and circled around his feet. Bill chuckled and rubbed the silky hair on her back.

"Bill?"

Recognition flashed through him. His hand stalled, and he looked up.

Jenn stood in the kitchen doorway, her wide hazel-green eyes full of questions.

"Hi." Suddenly his mouth felt dry as chalk.

"I wasn't sure if you were coming." She glanced around the room, sounding as uncertain as he felt.

"Yeah, I uh . . . wanted to bring Tilley a present." He stood and faced her. A thousand other things he wanted to say circled through his mind, but he remembered Wes's warning and held them back. He glanced down at the puppy. *Help me out, Lord. I feel like a fish out of water.*

"I named her Sophie," Jenn said softly.

He swallowed, and new strength flowed through him. Lifting his head, he met Jenn's gaze. "You must be taking good take of her. She looks great."

"I can't believe how much she's grown." Jenn stepped over a baby gate they'd set up to corral the puppy in the mudroom. She held out her hand. "Come here, Sophie." The puppy ran to her, and Jenn scooped her up in her arms. She laughed as Sophie squirmed and snuggled up close. "You're a little sweetheart, aren't you?" She kissed the dog on top of the head and then held her up so she could look into her face.

Bill grinned, his heart lifting. "Looks like you two are getting along pretty well."

"We are. She has a playful personality, but she's not too hyper." She looked up at him. "She cried a lot the first couple nights, so I let her sleep in my room. That seemed to help her settle down. I guess she just wanted to be close to me."

Bill nodded, fighting off a surge of longing. He knew it

was crazy, but he wished he could trade places with the dog, even if only for a little while.

Jenn gave the puppy another kiss then set her down. "Come on in. You're just in time for dessert."

He followed her through the kitchen and dining room and into the living room. Wes and Lauren greeted him. Toby jumped up from his spot on the couch and ran to slap Bill's hand and give him five.

"It's good to see you, Bill." Tilley stood and welcomed him with a hug. "We've missed you."

Bill exchanged a quick glance with Wes. "I've missed you, too." He handed Tilley the gift bag. "Happy birthday."

Her old blue eyes twinkled. "What's this?"

"I guess you'll have to look inside and see."

Tilley chuckled. "Let me get you a piece of cake first."

"No, that's okay. You go ahead and open your presents."

"I'll get it." Jenn hopped up and crossed to the dining room table. She cut him a thick slice of chocolate cake and scooped out a big spoonful of vanilla ice cream to go with it.

His mouth watered as she handed him the plate. "Thanks. This looks great."

"You're welcome." She sent him a sweet smile, then sat down across from him in an overstuffed chair that faced the couch.

"Open my present first!" Toby jumped up and handed his great aunt a medium-size square box wrapped in the Sunday comics. He hopped from one foot to the other watching her turn the box around in her hands.

"Toby, settle down," Lauren said. "You're going to jump on Aunt Tilley's toes."

"Okay." Toby stopped bouncing and leaned on the arm of Tilley's chair.

Tilley shook the box. "Hmmm, what could this be? Maybe it's a motorcycle or inflatable underwear!"

Toby giggled. "No, it's not that. It's a—"

"Shhh, don't tell." Wes winked at Toby. "Let her open it and see for herself."

Bill grinned and took a bite of cake. This is what he missed, the warmth of family and the fun of sharing moments like these.

Tilley opened the box and took out a beehive-shaped cookie jar. "Oh my, look at this! What a fun idea. Did you pick it out for me?" Toby nodded, and she kissed his cheek. "Thank you, sweetie. We'll have to make some cookies to fill it up."

"Yes!" Toby hopped up and down again reminding Bill of a rabbit with too much caffeine.

Lauren laid her hand on her son's shoulder and asked him to give Tilley the next gift.

Bill settled back on the couch, intending to watch Tilley, but his gaze drifted to Jenn. She wore a blue flowered skirt and a white shirt made of a silky-looking material. The shirt had long sleeves, but she'd rolled them up to her elbows, showing her slim wrists. He felt certain he'd never seen her wear that outfit before. She looked great, very feminine and appealing.

She looked up, and her gaze connected with his. She smiled again, her eyes shining with a happy light.

His heart clutched, and he quickly shifted his gaze away. What he really wanted to do was walk across the room, take her in his arms, and tell her how much he'd missed her. He doused that thought and fought to focus on the conversation between Tilley and Lauren.

A few minutes later, after Tilley had unwrapped all her gifts, Lauren offered everyone refills on coffee.

"Can I have some more cake?" Toby sent his mother a pleading look.

"I think one piece is enough, but you can have a little more ice cream if you want."

Toby smiled and nodded. Lauren spooned out another

small serving for him.

Jenn set aside her empty dessert plate. "Oh, I almost forgot, I have some good news."

"What's that?" Tilley asked.

"A reporter from the newspaper called. He wants to interview me."

"Wow, that's exciting." Lauren settled on the couch next to Wes.

A shadow of concern filled Wes's eyes. "What's his angle?" Wes was cautious of the media since the distorted story of his imprisonment in the Middle East had been splashed across national news magazines.

"He wants to write an article about me and take pictures of the furniture I've been painting."

Lauren set her coffee cup on the end table. "How did he find out about it?"

"His wife came in the gallery earlier this week. She's the one who bought the pie safe."

Bill's brows rose. "You mean the one we got at the flea market?"

Jenn nodded. "I guess he liked it, too, and now he wants to bring out a photographer and write a story."

"Great!" Lauren beamed. "So, when's he coming?"

"Tomorrow at two. I hope that's okay. I should've run it by you first."

"No, it's fine. It's your interview."

Jenn glanced at Bill as she got up. "I'll be right back." A couple minutes later, she came downstairs and handed Bill a white envelope. "This is your part of the money from selling the pie safe."

He stared at the envelope for a second then shook his head. "I can't take this, Jenn."

"But we agreed to split the money."

"All the work you put into it is what made it valuable. Please, keep this." He put the envelope in her hand.

"Use it to buy another piece of furniture or some more paint."

A slow smile lifted her lips, and appreciation glowed in her eyes. "Okay. Thanks. I'll reinvest it in another project."

He felt his heart swell. If only he could make her happy like that every day for the rest of his life.

But the truth rushed in, blowing away the dream. There was no chance of that happening unless God did a miracle in Jenn's heart.

Did he have the faith to wait for that? Was that what God wanted him to do? He didn't see many changes yet, just a few hints that her heart might be softening. But wasn't that what faith was all about . . . waiting and believing even though you don't see the answer yet?

CHAPTER 19

Jenn reached into the backseat of Lauren's car and pulled out the round metal container of brownies. She glanced across the parking lot at the nature center. Would she find Bill working in his office, or would he be off in the woods leading a group of children on an outing?

She'd planned to call before she drove over, but when she picked up the phone, her courage melted away. She decided it would be better to just show up. That way she wouldn't have to hear the indifference in his voice.

She straightened her light-green shirt and brushed a piece of lint off her beige Capri pants. A shiver passed through her even though it was a warm, sunny day. Why was she so nervous? This was just a friendly visit, a chance to reconnect and ask Bill for a little advice.

She scoffed at herself as she crossed the parking lot. It was more than that, and she knew it. She missed him terribly, and ever since the night of Tilley's birthday celebration, she hadn't been able to stop thinking about him. She was almost certain she'd felt a special connection between them that evening.

But if that was true, why didn't he call or come by? What

was keeping him away? Maybe she'd just imagined it because of her growing feelings for him.

She pushed open the front door and stepped inside. Her steps slowed as she looked at the mural on the wall opposite the entrance. Memories of the time she spent with Bill planning the project filtered through her mind and warmed her heart.

Clutching the brownie container, she surveyed the room looking for Bill, but she didn't see him among the dozen or so children and adults scattered around enjoying the interactive exhibits. She glanced into the quiet auditorium, but he wasn't there either.

Mandy and Troy walked into the room and spotted her. Mandy waved. "Hey, Jenn. Are you looking for Wes?"

Jenn's face warmed as she crossed toward them. "No, actually, I'm looking for Bill. Is he around?"

Troy nodded and pointed over his shoulder. "He's in the office. But I'll warn you, he's not in the best mood."

She thanked them and slipped down the hall, her stomach doing a nervous dance. She'd rarely seen Bill in a bad mood. What could be bothering him?

Bill's office door stood halfway open. She peeked in and saw him sitting at his desk, focusing on his computer.

She swallowed and knocked on the doorjamb.

He looked up. Surprise flashed in his eyes. "Jenn."

"Hi. I thought I'd stop by and bring you some brownies." She forced a smile and held out the container. Suddenly, her knees felt like limp noodles, and she wasn't sure how she would make them work.

"Wow, Thanks. That's nice." But his kind words didn't match his troubled expression.

Her face flamed as she crossed the room and set the container on his desk. He obviously wasn't happy to see her. When was she going to get the point and stop making a fool of herself?

He shifted in his chair. "Do you want to sit down?"

"Okay. Thanks." She took a seat facing the desk and tried to calm her jittery nerves. "So, did you see the article in the paper on Friday?"

A slight smile lifted one side of his mouth. "Yeah, that was amazing. They gave you most of the page and used all those photos."

Her tense muscles relaxed a little, and she returned his smile. "The gallery phone has been ringing off the hook. A lot of people are coming in and placing special orders. One lady even brought in an antique trunk she wants me to refinish and paint to match the colors scheme in her bedroom."

"Wow, all that from the article?"

She nodded. "Lauren's happy. Sales are twice what they were last week. We stayed up late last night talking about it." A tremor passed through her as she lifted her gaze and focused on him. "I was planning to go back to Oregon after the wedding, but . . . now I'm thinking about staying."

His eyes widened and flickered. "Really?"

"Yes." She studied his face, hope rising in her heart.

But the light in his eyes dimmed, and his cautious expression returned. "You're staying so you can work with Lauren?"

"Yes. She said I can cut my hours in the gallery after she gets back from their honeymoon. That'll give me more time to paint and work on those special orders. Maybe I can even develop it into my own business."

He leaned back in his chair and narrowed his eyes. "So, you're going to give up acting?"

His question threw her for a moment. "Well . . . I'm not sure. I might go back to it someday." Memories of the costumes she'd worn at the dinner theater flashed through her mind. How could she feel comfortable on stage knowing people were staring at her scars?

"So, you'll stay at Long Meadow with Lauren and Wes?"

"Until I save up enough for my own place."

He watched her with a neutral expression that didn't give a hint at his feelings.

"So . . . what do you think of the idea?"

He glanced off toward the window. "Why are you asking me?"

"Well, I'm not sure if I'm making the right decision. I was hoping you might help me think it through."

He crossed his arms and studied her again. "Okay, why wouldn't you want to stay?"

She bit her thumbnail, pondering his question. "I guess I feel guilty for not using my training as an actress. I spent a lot of money getting my degree and taking voice and dance lessons all those years.

"But then I think of how I feel when I'm painting, and I remember how peoples' faces light up when they look at my work." She fiddled with the hem of her shirt. "But what if all this interest in my painting dies down in a few days, and I never sell another piece?'

He leaned forward and rested his arms on the desk. "You have a special talent, Jenn. That's a gift from God. It may take some time to build your reputation, but if you get your work out there, I'm sure people are going to buy it. You can do this if you want to."

Her confidence rose as she listened, but then her doubts came flooding back. "But what if I'm a total flop? I can't sponge off Lauren and Wes forever."

He drummed his fingers on the desk for a moment and then looked across at her. "You want to know what I really think?"

"Yes." She held her breath, hoping he'd say he wanted her to stay, not just so she could paint and start her own business, but because he cared about her and wanted to see where their relationship would go.

He gave her a confident nod. "Whenever I have a tough decision to make, the first thing I do is pray. After that, I talk to people I trust and get their opinions and advice. Then I pray some more and ask God to show me the answer and make it so clear I can't miss it."

Jenn stared at him. That was all he had to say? He'd pray about it? Didn't he care if she stayed? Didn't he even have an opinion? She lowered her gaze to the floor, fighting back a rising flood of emotion.

She rose from the chair on trembling legs. "Thanks for the advice." She almost choked on the words, but she got them out, then spun away and strode out the door.

∽

Frustration churned Bill's stomach as he watched Jenn flee his office and disappear down the hall.

He'd obviously upset her again. It must have been his comments about praying for direction.

Closing his eyes, he sighed and ran his hand down his face. What was he supposed to say? She asked him what he would do, and he told her the truth. He'd never make an important decision like that without praying and waiting on the Lord. He wasn't going to lie to her, no matter how much she didn't want to hear it.

Recalling the stricken look on her face, he groaned and sank lower in his chair. It didn't matter if it was the truth. His timing was off—again! He'd spouted off an answer rather than praying and thinking through what was best for Jenn.

Maybe he'd call her later. But he quickly dismissed that idea. What was the point? The huge gulf separating them seemed to be getting wider every time they talked about anything more significant than the weather.

He leaned his head back and closed his eyes. *Father, I know You love Jenn even more than I do. You understand what's going on in her heart, and You know how to reach her. She needs you, Lord. Show me what you want me to do.*

There's got to be some way I can help her. Whatever it is, Lord, I'm willing.

He waited quietly, listening for some message or impression to settle in his heart. But the only sound he heard was the wind in the trees. Seconds ticked by as he stared out the window into the forest.

If he had no new direction, then he needed to hold on to the last answer he'd received: wait, pray, and give God time to work. Stay out of it. Nothing had changed. Her visit today had only made him more painfully aware of how much he missed her.

He glanced at the brownie container, and his shoulders sagged. She'd baked him a special treat, and he hadn't even looked inside or properly thanked her. She must think he was an ungrateful clod.

He pulled off the lid, and the luscious scent of chocolate filled the air. His mouth watered. He picked up a dark-brown, nut-studded brownie and found they were still soft and warm. He took a bite, leaned back in his chair and let the rich chocolate melt on his tongue. If her painting career didn't take off, she could definitely bake brownies for a living. He would be her best customer.

The phone on Bill's desk rang. He wiped his hand on his pants and picked it up. "Wild River Nature Center."

"Bill dear, is that you?"

"Hey, Mom." His shoulders tensed. His parents didn't usually call him at work. "Is everything okay?"

"Oh, Dad's a little under the weather with a cold, but other than that, we're all right."

"Sorry he's sick. Tell him I'll be praying for him." Bill took a second brownie from the container. "So, what's up?"

"I just had a call from Arleta Wilkins. Her nephew Steve works at Hawk Mountain."

"At the nature center?" Memories flooded back, making him smile. He'd seen his first eagle on Hawk Mountain when he was eight. He learned how to handle a canoe there, track animals, and mark a trail. The summer he turned sixteen he volunteered and had his first taste of teaching others about the wonder of God's creation.

His mother's voice broke through his memories. "The director of the nature center is retiring soon. They'll be looking for someone to replace him."

Bill sat up. "Are you sure about that?"

"I guess it's all still hush, hush. But Steve said it's probably not too soon to send a résumé."

Bill glanced around his office. Should he apply? What about his work here? He'd invested almost four years building the programs at Wild River. He had a dedicated staff and good group of volunteers. Under his guidance they'd won the Silver Eagle award for excellence in environmental education. He was proud of those accomplishments. Besides his job he had a great church and good friends. Immediately, Jenn's face flashed across his mind. "Thanks for the heads up, Mom. But I don't—"

"Please, Bill. Just think about it. It would be wonderful to have you back in North Carolina. It's been months since you've been home."

He rubbed the back of his neck. "I know. I'm sorry. Spring and summer are always a busy time around here."

"I hope you're planning to come home for the holidays. It wasn't the same without you last year."

His mom really knew how to heap on the guilt. "I'll be there for Thanksgiving. But I'm not sure about Christmas. I haven't worked on the schedule for December yet."

"If you took that position at Hawk Mountain you could come home anytime you like. Why don't you just call and talk to the people up there?"

He rubbed his jaw, trying to come up with an answer. But he knew she wouldn't be satisfied until he agreed to make the call.

"I know you love Vermont," his mom continued, "but the Hawk Mountain center is twice the size of Wild River. The salary is probably higher, plus you'd be closer to family . . . and there's no price you can put on that."

"It sounds great, Mom. And you know I love you and Dad, but I'm settled here. I own a house, and I'm involved at my church."

"But your dad and I miss you, and we're not going to be around forever, you know."

He held back a chuckle. "You're not exactly on your deathbeds yet."

His mother gasped. "Of course not. I didn't mean that. I just wish you lived nearby so we could see you more often." She waited for his reply and then sighed. "Okay. I guess I better go fix your dad some lunch. You take care, honey. And let me know what they say when you call up to Hawk Mountain."

He grinned and shook his head as he told his mom goodbye. She never gave up. Tilting back in his chair, his thoughts drifted back to Jenn.

He'd tried his best to stay away from her, but in a small town with common friends and activities, it was more difficult than he expected. Whether he was with her or not, he still cared, much more than he should if there was no future for them.

He released a weary sigh, recalling the night Wes had told him to back off and stop pursuing Jenn. He'd known the truth then. He couldn't just walk away and forget about her. He'd have to leave the state before that would happen.

That thought made him sit up straight.

Leave Vermont? Was that the answer? Could the opening at Hawk Mountain be a sign that God wanted him to let Jenn go and move on? He clamped his jaw against the pain twisting through him. That couldn't be right. Surely, God didn't expect him to give up Jenn and everything he had here, did He?

He closed his eyes, pushing those thoughts away. He didn't have to decide right now. His best friend was getting married in a few days. He needed to focus on helping Wes and Lauren. But he would have to face this issue soon. Was he willing to go if God called him back to North Carolina?

CHAPTER 20

Soft organ music floated toward Jenn as she entered the church foyer. Her long blue dress swished against her legs, and the scent of roses from her bouquet drifted in the air around her.

Three last minute wedding guests slipped past and entered the sanctuary through the side door. Jenn glanced at Julia and Lauren. Their faces glowed and their eyes sparkled. They looked as lovely as any models she'd seen in the bridal magazines she'd scanned in the last few weeks.

If only she felt as confident and radiant.

A tremor passed through her as she approached the main doors to the sanctuary. She hated being the first one to walk down the aisle, and knowing Bill stood up front next to her brother would make it even harder.

He had remained distant even after she visited him at the nature center. Telling him she wanted to stay in Vermont didn't seem to make any difference to him. Last night, during the wedding rehearsal and dinner afterward, he'd barely acknowledged her.

She silently scolded herself. This was no time to worry about seeing Bill. She was here today for Wes and Lauren. She just wouldn't look at him. That was the only way she'd make it through this ceremony without doing something awful and embarrassing herself, like breaking down in tears.

Clutching her bouquet, she turned to Julia. "Promise me you won't wait too long."

Julia smiled. "Don't worry. I'll be right behind you."

Marie Shelton, pastor Dan's wife, leaned toward Jenn. "Are you ready, dear?"

Jenn nodded though her knees felt weak and wobbly.

"All right then. Listen for the music, then take it nice and slow, just like we practiced last night." Marie gave Jenn a confident nod and opened the double doors.

The sight of the crowded sanctuary sent a shiver racing down her back. She lifted her chin and looked straight ahead, trying to quiet her dancing stomach. The organist transitioned into the processional, and she stepped through the doorway.

All eyes turned toward her. She swallowed and focused on her brother standing at the front of the church. He looked incredibly handsome in his black tux with a single white rose pined on his lapel. Smiling, he encouraged her forward with his eyes.

Forcing a stiff smile in return, she began her long journey down the aisle. Wes deserved to be happy today. And she would do whatever it took to make that happen, even though she felt like a bug under a microscope with 135 pairs of eyes staring at her.

A few seconds later, Wes broke eye contact and looked past her shoulder. Julia must have made her entrance because everyone turned toward the back of the church.

Jenn blew out a shaky breath, reminding herself to stay focused on Wes. But her gaze drifted to the right and connected with Bill's.

A look of awe and tenderness filled his expression as he watched her approach.

Jenn blinked and checked once more. Was he simply

moved by the emotion of the moment, or did his reaction reveal something deeper? She glanced away, fearful he would see her response, and read her thoughts.

She finally reached the front of the church, but before she took her place, she cast one more glance at Bill. His gaze remained on her even though Julia followed a few steps behind, and Toby fidgeted right in front of him.

Jenn turned and faced the guests, her mind spinning with confusion. Julia took her place beside her, and the first notes of the bridal processional rang out.

Tilley stood and the other guests rose to their feet. Cameras flashed and everyone turned to catch a glimpse of Lauren as she floated down the aisle, her face alight with love, her eyes fixed on Wes.

Adoration glowed on Wes's face as he took Lauren's hand and together they turned to face Pastor Dan.

Jenn's throat burned. She tried to hold back her tears, but a few spilled over and ran down her cheeks. Wes and Lauren looked so happy, so in love. And she knew it was true. She'd watched them closely over the last few weeks. Even during the hectic days leading up to the wedding the love and respect they showed each other amazed her.

Would she ever experience a love like that, one that connected her heart-to-heart with a man who would be committed to her for life? She closed her eyes to keep from looking at Bill again.

Pastor Dan's warm, steady voice welcomed everyone and then led them in prayer. Jenn listened carefully as he read two Bible passages about love.

His comments were personal and meaningful, and sincerity shone in his eyes as he spoke. "The type of love and commitment Wes and Lauren share is rare in our world today. They are promising to serve one another and honor one another above themselves, to put the other's interests above their own, and to always seek the highest and best for each other. That kind of love takes humility and sacrifice." His gaze traveled around the room, giving everyone time to consider his words. "And that is at the heart of the promises they make today."

Jenn looked down at her bouquet. Had she loved Phillip like that? Did she even know what it meant to place someone else's desires and plans above her own? What about sacrifice and service? She'd never really thought of love like that before.

The commitment Pastor Dan talked about was not a fifty-fifty arrangement where each one waited for the other to do his or her part. He spoke of a total commitment motivated by unconditional love that gave one hundred percent without waiting to see what the other person would give.

That kind of relationship sounded risky, but wouldn't it be amazing to be loved like that?

Pastor Dan glanced at Lauren and then Wes. "This kind of love is only possible if you are directly connected to Jesus Christ, the source of true love. As we grow in our relationship with Him and experience more of Him in our lives, then we will have a never-ending river of love that can flow through us to our mate, our children, our friends, and all we meet."

Longing stirred in Jenn's heart. She looked across the sanctuary at a stained glass window that pictured Jesus as the good shepherd tenderly carrying a lamb in his arms while several other sheep followed Him along the path.

Her throat tightened. How would it feel to be held like that, to be back in His care?

But it had been so long since she had prayed or acknowledged Him. Would He even want her back . . . or was it too late?

A story she had read in the Bible the night before replayed in her mind. It told of the shepherd leaving the ninety-nine sheep and going to look for the one that was lost and needed his help. The memory warmed her heart with a secret knowing. He was searching for her now, calling her home to His arms.

Pastor Dan's words brought her focus back to the ceremony as he led Wes and Lauren through their vows and the exchange of rings. Then they walked forward and lit a unity candle while a young couple sang a song about climbing the hills together. Pastor Dan prayed the final prayer. Then, with a broad grin, he pronounced them man and wife and invited Wes to kiss his bride.

Jenn bit her lip as she watched them embrace and exchange the sweetest kiss.

Pastor Dan beamed. "Let me be the first to introduce to you Mr. and Mrs. Wesley Evans."

The organist began the triumphant recessional, and everyone clapped and rose to their feet. With smiles wreathing their faces, Lauren took Wes's arm and they walked up the aisle together.

Julia stepped forward to meet Bill and slipped her arm through his. She smiled up at him, her blue eyes bright. But Bill's gaze flickered to Jenn. It only lasted a second, and Jenn suspected no one else had seen it. Then he turned and walked away with Julia. People smiled and nodded as they passed.

"Aren't they a lovely couple," an elderly woman in the second row said as she watched Bill and Julia pass.

Jenn's stomach tumbled. She forced a shaky smile, took Toby's hand, and followed Bill and Julia out of the sanctuary.

∼

JENN SIPPED SPARKLING cider from a fluted goblet and glanced up at the big white tent sheltering the reception guests. The Wild River Resort lawn had been transformed into a beautiful reception area. Round tables for eight were set with white china, sparking crystal and blue napkins. Overflowing bouquets of white roses, blue delphiniums, and purple orchids sat in the center of each table.

Soft music played in the background while a roving photographer clicked candid shots of people as they moved through the buffet line. Most of the guests had already filled their plates and returned to their seats to enjoy the delicious dinner.

Jenn set her goblet down and released a soft sigh. A melancholy mood had settled over her now that the ceremony had ended and the reception was winding down. In less than an hour Wes and Lauren would leave for their honeymoon, and she would stay behind to work in the gallery and help Tilley care for Toby.

She was glad she could do it, really she was . . . but somehow she couldn't help feeling deflated. She toyed with her stuffed chicken breast and pushed her plate aside. Glancing down the long head table past Toby, Lauren and Wes, she focused on Julia and Bill seated together at the other end of the table.

Bill had taken off his jacket and loosened his tie, but he still looked as handsome as ever. He turned to Julia. She flashed a quick smile and then laughed at something he said.

Jenn strained to listen, but with the music and conversation of the other guests swirling around her, she couldn't make out their words.

Julia leaned closer to Bill, laid her hand on his arm, and whispered in his ear. He nodded and sat back with an amused expression on his face. Then he shifted his gaze to Jenn and sent her a quick smile.

Jenn pulled in a sharp breath. The nerve! Flirting with Julia one second and with her the next.

She scooted her chair back, intending to snatch her purse and make a quick exit to the ladies' room, but Toby turned and banged into her. His cold cider splashed her shoulder.

Toby gasped and looked at her with wide eyes. "Sorry, Aunty Jenn."

"It's okay." Her cheeks burned as she grabbed a cloth napkin and tried to blot up the mess. She deserved this for watching Bill and not paying attention.

Lauren turned toward them. "What happened?"

"It's just a little spill." But Jenn could feel the cider dripping down her arm. She'd have to take off her jacket to wipe up the sticky mess.

"I'm sorry, Jenn." Sympathy filled Lauren's voice. "Do you need some more napkins?"

"No, I think I'll go rinse off." She reached under the table for her purse, keeping an eye on Toby this time.

Someone began tapping the side of a glass with his spoon. Soon the clinking chorus rose and filled the tent. Wes turned to Lauren and gave her a lingering kiss. The guests clapped and cheered.

Jenn swallowed as she watched them, then turned and slipped away from the tent. When she reached the stone pathway leading to the back entrance to the lodge, she heard familiar voices. Looking over her shoulder, she spotted Bill and Julia hurrying from the tent together. Julia had taken off her jacket, and the late afternoon sun splashed across her tanned shoulders. The sound of their laughter floated back to Jenn as they slipped around the side of the building.

Hot irritation flashed through her, quickly followed by a cooling wave of regret. She couldn't stay angry with them. She liked them both too much. Besides, Bill hadn't made any promises to her. He was free to take off with whomever he wanted.

Then why was she so upset?

Because she liked him much more than she'd been willing to admit to herself or anyone else. But it was too late to do anything about it now. She'd lost him to Julia.

No, she hadn't lost him . . . because she'd never had him. He'd always only been her friend, her kind, caring, wonderful friend. But now, even their friendship seemed to be slipping away.

She trudged up the steps and pushed open the heavy glass door. Cool air conditioning sent a shiver up her back as she stepped into the lodge lobby. She followed the signs to the restroom and made her way to a private sink in the shower area, hoping she could avoid anyone else.

As she reached to turn on the water, she heard the bathroom door open. She peeked around the corner and saw two young teens walk in.

The first girl, a short blond who looked about fifteen, pulled a tube of lip-gloss from her purse. "Did you see Brian Shelton hanging out with Mandy by the punch table?"

The other girl nodded and flipped her long dark hair over her shoulder. "I can't believe she won't go out with him. What is her problem?"

"I don't know. Everyone in youth group thinks he is so cool. I'd die if he ever asked me out."

Jenn slipped back around the corner, remembering her own high school escapades.

"Did you see the way my aunt Julia was hanging out with the best man?"

Jenn froze, her heart hammering.

"You mean Bill Morgan?"

"Yes. Isn't he a dream?"

The first girl sighed. "I could hardly keep my mind on what he was saying the last time our class went out to the nature center."

"My mom said my aunt has liked him forever."

"Really? I wonder why it's taken them so long to get together. Your aunt is gorgeous."

"I know. I guess some guys are just clueless." Both girls laughed.

Perspiration dotted Jenn's forehead as she rinsed the sticky juice off her arm and hands.

"Hey, remember the way they were squirting each other and goofing around when they helped out at the youth group car wash?"

The other girl gasped. "That's right. I should've guessed what was going on then."

"They look so cute together. Do you think they'll get married next?"

"Probably. My mom says my aunt wants a family in the worst way."

"She lives with your grandpa, right?"

"Yeah, but that's not the same as having a husband and kids."

"Especially a cute husband like Bill Morgan. I bet their kids will be adorable."

Jenn gulped and tried to slow her racing heart. This was not happening. These girls didn't know what they were talking about. Bill and Julia were not about to get engaged, were they? She tried to force those thoughts away, but painful questions rose and took their place. Was that why Bill never came to see her anymore? Why hadn't she heard anything about it?

Jenn crossed behind the girls and pulled out a paper towel to dry her hands. The girls exchanged wary glances as they continued to primp and brush their hair.

The bathroom door flew open and another teenage girl leaned in. "You guys better hurry up. Lauren's going to throw the bouquet any minute."

The brunette grabbed her purse off the counter. "Let's go." The two girls hustled out the door, leaving Jenn staring at her pale reflection in the mirror.

CHAPTER 21

*B*ill stuffed the leftover crape paper streamers in the plastic bag and walked toward the reception tent. Julia had stayed behind to finish attaching the Just Married sign to the rear window of Wes's car. But he needed to get back. Hopefully, he could catch a few minutes with Jenn. He'd held back and given her plenty of space, but there was something he had to tell her, and it couldn't wait.

Out of the corner of his eye, he caught a flash of blue. Turning, he saw Jenn hurry down the lodge steps and head toward the parking lot.

His heartbeat kicked up a notch. He took off at a jog and caught up with her near the end of the first row of cars. "Hey, where are you going? The party's not over yet."

"I'm not feeling well." She kept walking. "I'm going back to the house."

Concern rose and tightened his chest. He moved around in front of her. "I'll drive you."

"No, I'm okay. I'm just not in the mood for all this." She stepped to the right.

He countered and blocked her path. "What happened?"

His gaze darted to her shoulder and held. He'd never seen these deeper scars with the square patch of lighter skin grafted over them. He clenched his hands and steeled himself against the response coursing through him. "Did someone say something?"

She looked away. "No, I'm just tired. I want to go home."

"Come on. You can tell me." He forced a teasing grin. "I know that's not it."

Color flooded her cheeks, and her eyes flashed. "Why should you care? Why don't you just go back and enjoy the rest of the reception with Julia?"

"What?" Shockwaves rippled through him.

"Look, it's obvious what's going on. Every time I turn around someone is talking about you and Julia and how perfect you are together. You go to the same church, you have the same friends, you're the best man, she's the maid of honor." She lifted her hands. "It makes sense."

"That's what's bothering you?" Her jealousy tickled him more than it should have, and he couldn't keep the smile out of his voice.

"Never mind!" She glared at him and spun away.

"Whoa." He reached for her arm. "I'm sorry. I shouldn't be joking around about this." He waited until she looked him in the eyes. "There's nothing between Julia and me."

"Oh, is that right?" She pulled her arm away. "Then why did you just sneak off with her?"

He stared at her a second, trying to figure out what she meant. Then it dawned on him, and he opened his mouth to explain, but she held up her hand to stop him.

"Don't deny it. I saw you." The hurt in her eyes stole all the humor from the situation.

"We were decorating Wes's car."

Her eyes widened for a split second, then she narrowed them, distrust settling over her features.

"Jenn, I promise you, I'm not interested in Julia. I never have been. She's great girl, but she's just not . . ." How could he explain it? There was no connection, no spark, nothing like what he felt when he was around Jenn.

"Not what?" A hopeful light tinged with longing shone in Jenn's eyes.

The truth burned in his throat and became a silent plea for help. A cooling breeze blew past, helping him focus, giving him strength. "She's not the right one for me."

Jenn searched his face, waiting for him to say more. When he didn't, she sighed and rubbed her forehead, shielding her eyes from him. "I'm sorry. I'm just so confused. After the fourth of July, I thought . . ."

Pain twisted through him. "Yeah, I'm a little confused myself." He shoved his hands in his pants pockets, feeling the weight of the next words he would say. "I have something I need to tell you."

She looked up, a wary look in her eyes. "What?"

He straightened his shoulders, wishing there was some other way, but this was the path he felt called to follow, though it was the last one he would've chosen. "I applied for a job in North Carolina. I'm going down for an interview on the twenty-first."

Her face paled. "Do Wes and Lauren know?"

"I didn't want to say anything before the wedding. There'll be plenty of time to talk to them when they get back if it all works out." But the people at Hawk Mountain were paying for him to fly down for this interview, so he knew they were serious.

"But I don't understand. Why would you leave?"

He clenched his jaw and looked away. He knew she cared, but he hadn't realized how much. He had to clear his throat before he could speak. "My parents are getting older. I'd like to be closer so I can help them out a little more."

With a shaky hand she tucked a strand of hair behind her ear. "So, this is about being closer to home and helping your parents?"

He swallowed and nodded, hating that he had to keep the rest of the truth from her. But she wouldn't understand. What could he say? She wasn't spiritual enough? That would be a huge insult and hurt her more than he already had.

She looked up at him with sorrowful, pleading eyes.

Doubt hit and shook him to the core. Had he truly heard from the Lord? Was he making a huge mistake? What if he just took her in his arms right now and told her he loved her? Eventually she'd come around and grow to love the Lord, wouldn't she?

A cloud passed over the sun, sending a shadow rushing toward them, sealing his choice.

He couldn't stay. There was no future for them. Love and commitment to God formed the bond that held a relationship together through good times and bad. Praying together, serving together, sharing common goals and values, that was what made a marriage work. He knew it was true, but he'd never known how hard it could be to obey those principles.

"I'm sorry Jenn." A boulder lodged in his throat, and he had to force out the next words. "I never meant to hurt you."

A tear slipped down her cheek, and an ocean of pain filled her eyes. Without another word, she turned and walked away.

This time, he let her go.

~

THUNDER RUMBLED overhead and shook the house. Raindrops splattered against Jenn's bedroom window. A streak of lightning flashed as she reached to lower the blinds. Goose bumps raced up her arms. She dropped the blinds with a snap, rubbed her arms and returned to her cozy spot on the bed.

Twelve days had passed since Wes and Lauren's wedding. Jenn had spent the time working in the gallery, painting, and helping Tilley keep Toby out of trouble. Most evenings she settled in her room to read a chapter or two in the Bible Lauren had given her. After she finished, she poured out her thoughts and questions on the pages of her journal.

Picking up the Bible again, she flipped to the fourteenth chapter of John where she'd left off.

Jesus was an amazing man full of purpose and compassion, not a weak pawn as one of her college professors had insisted. His teaching captivated her, and her heart softened each time she read how He healed the sick and handicapped or showed love to the poor and lonely. He appreciated people who asked honest questions and those who demonstrated their faith by their actions. Most of all, He seemed to be looking for those who were willing to follow God with their whole heart.

She lay back on her pillows and closed her eyes. She had been poor and lonely when she came to Vermont almost five months ago. Wes, Lauren and Tilley had welcomed her into their home and family and shown her so much love. She smiled, remembering the way Wes and Lauren thanked her for helping with the wedding before they left for their honeymoon. Wes's last words were, "You know Lauren and I love you." Then they'd hugged her and kissed her goodbye.

And Bill . . . her heart ached as she thought of him. Was he still in North Carolina? Had he accepted the job that would take him so far away from her? She hadn't seen him since the wedding, though she thought of him every day and spent too much time dreaming of ways for them to connect again when he got back.

The last two Sundays she'd gone to church with Tilley, hoping she would run into him there, but for some reason, she hadn't. The prospect of seeing Bill hadn't been her only motivation for attending. She'd enjoyed getting to know

Pastor Dan and his wife at the wedding, and she liked the way he explained the Bible and made it easy for her to understand. That seemed to ease the ache in her heart and help her feel closer to God.

She'd been surprised to learn so many people she'd met at the wedding attended the church. Rather than feeling out of place, they'd made her feel welcome.

If only Bill had been there.

She shook her head and released a deep sigh. Even though it hadn't worked out between them, she would always be grateful for his caring friendship, his kindness and acceptance. He looked past the surface into her heart, to who she really was. He had taught her so much by his example and the way he'd lived out his faith in his daily life. Jenn smiled through tears.

When she thought of Jesus, she imagined he looked a lot like Bill.

She picked up her journal and turned to a new page. Dear Father, thank you for drawing me back to You. Thank You for the people You've sent to show me what it means to love You and follow You. There are a lot of things I don't understand about my life and all that's happened, like why I had to go through the fire. But I believe You'll help me work that out in my heart and show me what I need to learn from that experience.

I'm not sure what you want me to do with my life. Help me to trust You and give me courage to follow You no matter what happens. And please take care of Bill wherever he is tonight.

She hesitated, wondering if she could ask God to make Bill stay in Vermont. Slowly, she shook her head and let that idea go. She didn't want to be selfish anymore. True love, like Pastor Dan said, meant thinking about what was best for the other person, putting their needs above your own.

I wish he could stay. That's what I really want. But if it's best for him to go to North Carolina, then I pray you'll give him that new job, and You'll help me let go of the dream of us being together some day. Though her heart ached at that thought, she whispered, "Amen," and closed her journal.

CHAPTER 22

Sunlight beamed across the gallery's oak plank floor. The wood added a warm touch to the decor, but it needed a good sweeping each evening before they closed. Jenn didn't mind. The gentle rhythm of the broom swishing across the floorboards soothed her spirit.

It had been a busy afternoon. A vanload of tourists came in just after lunch and kept her hopping for over an hour as they asked questions and lined up to pay for their purchases. A little after three, the woman who'd brought in the antique trunk to be refinished returned to pick it up. She raved about Jenn's work and didn't even bat an eyelash when she looked at the bill.

Jenn smiled as she knelt with the dustpan in her hand. Lauren would be pleased when she returned on Sunday and saw the sales totals for the last two weeks.

She finished sweeping and walked to the back of the gallery where she hung the broom and dustpan in the closet. As she flipped off the closet light, she heard the front door open. Her heartbeat picked up. Could it be Bill? She hadn't seen him since the wedding, and she couldn't squelch the hope rising in her heart as she hurried back through the gallery and peeked around the stairwell.

Her spirits deflated when she spotted a man with blond hair standing with his back to her, studying a shelf of antique candleholders. She stepped out. "Can I help you find something?"

The man turned and smiled. "Hello, darling."

Jenn froze and stared at him, her stomach dropping to her toes. "Phillip?"

"Of course. You were expecting someone else?" He quirked one eyebrow, looking amused.

"What . . . what are you doing here? How did you find me?"

"You did make that difficult." His smile faded. "I've been worried about you, Jenn. Why didn't you tell me where you were going?"

She sent him a glance of utter disbelief. "I didn't think you wanted—"

"I've been searching for you for months. The other night I Googled your name again and found the newspaper article about your work here at the gallery." His smile resurfaced. "At first I didn't think it could be the same Jennifer Evans. But then I saw the photos, and I knew I'd found you." He stepped closer and slid his hand down her arm. "I've missed you, Jenn, more than I can say."

She stiffened at his touch.

He leaned back and searched her face. "What's wrong? I came all this way. I thought you'd be happy to see me."

"After the way you reacted at the hospital, I thought it was over between us."

His eyes widened, and he shook his head. "I just needed time to think it through and adjust to . . . everything. You have to understand, seeing you like that was a bit of a shock for me."

It had been a terrible shock for her, too. And his disappearance had left her to deal with it alone. She smoothed her sleeve over her scarred arm, fighting off a confused mixture of emotions. Could she have misread his response at the hospital? Had the trauma of the fire and the medication distorted her thinking?

She looked up and met his gaze. "But you never came back after the first night."

He huffed and lifted his hands. "I tried to call you. Didn't you get my messages?"

She shook her head, remembering the painful days following the fire. After she left the hospital, she'd stayed with her friend Natalie, then she'd gone to Stacey's. Phillip wouldn't have known how to reach her there. Could she have misjudged him? Was this whole misunderstanding her fault?

He grasped her hand. "Listen, darling, that's all behind us now. We've found each other again. That's what matters, that and making plans for the future."

Apprehension prickled through her. "What do you mean?"

His smile spread wider. "I want you to come back to Oregon with me."

Stunned, she stared at him.

"Auditions start Wednesday for the next show, and I think you'd be perfect for the lead."

She blinked. "The lead?"

He nodded. "I already spoke to Donavan about it. He's very interested."

He'd talked to the director for her? They wanted her to audition? Her heart lifted, but reality brought her back to earth. "I appreciate you speaking to Donavan, but I don't see how I could afford to move back right now. I don't have enough money to rent an apartment or replace my car."

He waved away her words. "Don't worry about that. You can stay with me. I'll drive you anywhere you need to go."

He slipped his arms around her shoulder and kissed her cheek. "I'll take care of everything."

A dizzy, lightheaded feeling washed over her. Was that what she wanted—a live-in relationship with Phillip? More uncomfortable questions rose in her mind. She slipped out of his embrace. "I don't think that would be a good idea for either of us."

"Why not? It's the perfect solution. You can come back to Oregon, and we can work together doing what we love." He grinned and cocked one eyebrow. "And maybe we can finally set a wedding date."

Tingles zinged along her nerves. "You're serious? You still want to get married?"

"Of course. Missing you all these months makes me realize how wrong I was to hold off on planning the wedding." He leaned down and looked into her eyes. "I want us to be together, Jenn."

∽

Bill pulled into the driveway at Long Meadow and parked between the house and barn. A silver convertible sat in the spot closest to the gallery's front door. With a slight frown, he glanced at his watch. Jenn should have closed by now. He shrugged off that thought. She was probably helping one last customer with a purchase before she locked up for the night.

He grabbed his keys, climbed out of the truck, and took a moment to stretch. He'd returned from his three-day trip to North Carolina that morning, and he still felt a little stiff from being cooped up in the airplane.

The interview had gone well. They'd practically handed him the job on the spot. The board would meet tonight for the final vote, then they promised to call. When the offer came through, he wouldn't be able to delay his decision much longer.

He lifted his gaze to the sky. Father, please show me what to do. I don't want to leave Vermont, but I'm willing to take that job at Hawk Mountain if that's what You want for me.

He glanced at the gallery door, wishing Jenn would walk outside and into his arms. He silenced that thought and refocused on his prayer.

Please help her work through the issues in her past so she can learn to trust You and love You with her whole heart. I'd turn down that job in a minute if You'd just give me one little sign that she's coming around. That would be enough for me.

His shoulders relaxed as a growing sense of hope filled him. He'd been praying non-stop for Jenn, asking God to touch her in new and deeper ways. He had no idea how God would do it, but he didn't doubt He could.

He walked toward the barn certain it was time to see her, time to talk. Opening the screen door, he stepped from bright sunshine into the gallery's shady interior. He hesitated on the threshold, waiting for his eyes to adjust. The room came into focus, and a shockwave jolted through him.

A man he'd never seen before held Jenn in his arms, and there was no mistaking the look of possession on the man's face.

A surge of confusion and betrayal flooded Bill. This was crazy! How could she fall in love with someone else? Who was this guy, anyway?

The screen door banged closed behind Bill. The man dropped his hold on Jenn and stepped back.

She turned, her eyes widened, and the color drained from her face. "Bill, you're back."

He nodded solemnly. "I got in this morning."

The blond man lifted his eyebrows and shot Jenn a questioning look.

"Phillip, this is Bill Morgan." Her gaze darted back and forth between them. "He's . . . he was my brother's roommate."

Bill's stomach churned. So that's all he was to her. But whose fault was that? He was the one who hadn't told her how he felt or what truly separated them.

"Bill, this is Phillip Reynolds."

The name hit him like a slap in the face. "From Oregon?"

She pressed her lips together and nodded, her face flushing.

Bill focused on Phillip and steeled his gaze. "So, what are you doing here?"

Surprise flashed in Phillip's gray eyes, but he quickly masked it. "I've come to bring Jenn home to Oregon with me." He smiled as though there was no doubt in his mind that she'd go with him. "She has a promising career waiting to take off, and a devoted fiancé eager to marry her."

Bill's anger bubbled closer to the surface. How could Phillip call himself a devoted fiancé? Where had he been all these months? He shifted his gaze to Jenn. "You want to go back to Oregon with him?" She sent him a pleading look that totally baffled him.

Phillip slipped his arm around her shoulder. "Of course she does. In just a few days Jenn has an opportunity to audition for the lead in an important production. It could open all kinds of doors for her."

"You're going back to acting?" Bill couldn't keep the incredulous tone out of his voice.

Jenn clasped her hands. "Well, I—"

"Jenn has exceptional talent and training. It would be foolish for her—"

"Hold on," Bill said, lifting his hand. "She's not a puppet. You can't just pull some strings and think you can control her."

"That's not what I am trying to do." Color rose in Phillip's face. "Jenn's happiness is my main concern."

Bill huffed. "Since when are you an authority on what makes Jenn happy?"

"She did accept my proposal. I'd say that gives me a pretty good idea."

"Oh, yeah, right," Bill sputtered.

"Please, stop." Jenn stepped between them. "You're talking about me like I'm not in the room."

Phillip straightened and took her hand. "I'm sorry, darling. Of course you're here. And I'm sure you can explain everything to . . ." He turned to Bill with a haughty lift of his eyebrows. "What was your name?"

"Bill Morgan," he ground out, glaring at Phillip. How could she even consider going anywhere with this pompous jerk? Her happiness was the last thing on his mind. Couldn't she see he was full of himself?

She slipped her hand out of Phillip's grip. "Phillip just got here. We've only had a few minutes to talk. I haven't made up my mind about anything yet."

Bill nodded, feeling as if he'd just scored a hard-won point. At least she wasn't ready to hop on a plane tonight. There was still a chance to convince her to stay. But he had no idea how he was going to do that.

"Why don't I walk you out to your truck," she said.

Bill shot one more glaring look at Phillip before he turned and followed Jenn out the door. As soon as the screen closed behind him, he strode up beside her. "So, he just shows up here after four months and expects you to take off with him?"

Jenn walked down the gravel drive a few more steps before she stopped in the shade of a maple tree. "It's been five months, actually. But I think that may be my fault."

Bill squinted, trying to catch her meaning.

"After the fire, I was in shock and they gave me a lot of pain medication. I think I might have misunderstood Phillip's reaction."

Bill slowly shook his head. "I don't believe this."

Her eyes widened. "What?"

"He deserted you, Jenn, when you needed him most. Now you're blaming yourself and defending him? That's crazy!"

Hurt filled her expression. "You don't understand. We were both upset that night. We said things we didn't mean."

"Okay, but that's no excuse for him dropping off the face of the earth. He should've been there for you."

"He said he needed time to adjust and process everything."

Bill groaned and rubbed the back of his neck. Couldn't she see that was a totally lame excuse?

"I should've called him and talked things over when I got out of the hospital, but I was so confused. I stayed with friends for a while, then I came up here without telling him where I was going. He says he's been looking for me ever since."

"And you believe him?"

"Well, he's here isn't he?" She lifted her chin, and a stubborn glint shone in her eyes.

"Yes, but that doesn't mean you should pack your bags and fly off with him."

"He says he wants to marry me."

Bill tossed his hand in the air. "Oh, yeah, I bet he does."

"What?" she snapped. "You don't think anyone in their right mind would want to marry me?"

"No, that's not what I meant." He rubbed his forehead, trying to straighten out his thoughts. Why had Phillip shown up now? It didn't make sense. There must be more to it than a simple change of heart. "I don't think you should trust him."

"Why would you say that? You don't even know him."

"Well, he's an actor, isn't he?"

"What's that got to do with it?"

"How can you trust someone who's paid to play a part?"

She narrowed her eyes. "Bill, I'm an actor, just like Phillip."

"No. You're nothing like him." Bill's thoughts raced

around in a circle. He wasn't convincing her of anything except that he was a little crazy.

"I don't understand why you're giving me such a hard time. Why should you care if I go back to Oregon? You're leaving."

He groaned. "Come on, Jenn."

"What? You want me to turn down a perfectly good marriage proposal just because it means moving across country?"

He rubbed his forehead, totally stumped at how to explain things to her. But he had to say something. "Please, just . . . don't rush into this. At least wait until Wes and Lauren come home. Talk it over with them. See what they say."

She crossed her arms and stared off toward the house, the struggle evident on her face. "I promised Wes and Lauren I'd keep the gallery open. I won't leave before they get back."

Two days. That wasn't nearly enough time to convince her to stay, especially with Phillip hanging around every minute. Doubts came rushing in, and cold sweat broke out on his forehead. Jenn deserved to get married and have a family someday, but the thought of her marrying Phillip turned his stomach. How could a guy like that be good for her? He had an attitude as big as a house, and he wanted to take her away from Vermont and the only family she had left.

But what if he was wrong about Phillip? What if he was being totally selfish? He swallowed and looked at Jenn. "Do you love him?"

She pressed her lips together, lowering her gaze. "I thought I did. But so much has happened. I'm not sure anymore."

Her response sparked a tiny flame of hope. Maybe there was still a chance, at least to convince her to stay.

Phillip stepped out the front door of the gallery door, his eyes glued to them.

Bill tensed and looked back at Jenn. "Promise me you'll

give it more time before you turn your life upside down again."

Questions shimmered in her hazel eyes, but she nodded. "I'll wait until Sunday and talk to Wes and Lauren."

Bill nodded. That was enough for now.

CHAPTER 23

Saturday morning Jenn set the steaming plate of French toast and bacon on the table in front of Phillip. "Here you go."

"Thanks." Phillip looked up at her with an uneasy smile that didn't look too convincing.

Jenn took her plate from the counter and joined Phillip at the kitchen table. He had been acting strange ever since he arrived that morning. Was he still bothered because she'd asked him to stay at a nearby bed and breakfast last night? Or perhaps he would've rather gone out this morning instead of eating with Tilley and Toby. She wasn't sure, but for some reason she didn't mind him being a little uncomfortable. After all, he was the one who had just shown up yesterday with no warning.

Tilley bustled toward the table carrying a red ceramic bowl. "We have peaches with whipped cream or warm maple syrup."

Toby reached for the bowl. "I want peaches on mine."

"Hold your horses, young man." Tilley looked at him over the top of her glasses. "We're going to pray first."

"Sorry." He grinned and slipped his hands back in his lap.

"That's better." Tilley sat down and smiled across the table at Phillip. "Would you like to pray?"

Jenn stifled a little gasp.

Phillip's face flushed. "Well, I—"

"I'll pray." Jenn bowed her head and closed her eyes. "Dear God, thank you for our breakfast and for everyone around this table. Please be with us and watch over us today. Amen." Her cheeks flamed as she looked up.

Tilley wore a pleased smile as she poured orange juice into his glass. "So, Phillip, what are your plans for the day?"

"Well, I thought Jenn and I would take a drive and do a little exploring." He ladled maple syrup on his French toast. "I've never been to Vermont before."

Jenn swallowed and set her fork down. "I'm sorry, Phillip. I should've mentioned this last night. I'm working in the gallery today from ten to five."

He sent her a puzzled look. "Isn't there someone else who could fill in for you?"

"Not really. I'm the only one working until Lauren gets back."

"When is that?"

"Tomorrow around six. But we're closed on Sundays, so we can go for a drive after church if you like."

His eyebrows rose. "Church?"

She nodded, feeling a little surge of mirth at his surprised expression. She'd enjoyed going the last two weeks, and she didn't intend to miss tomorrow. "The service is over about twelve. So that gives us all afternoon. But I'd like to be here when Wes and Lauren get back."

"They're bringing me a surprise," Toby added, his smile spreading wider.

Phillip ignored Toby, and a frown settled on his forehead. "Can't you just close the gallery today? I'm sure you've worked extra hours while they're away."

She shook her head. "I couldn't do that. Saturday is always our busiest day."

Toby reached across and took another piece of bacon from the serving platter. As he brought it back to his plate, his hand bumped Phillip's juice glass and knocked it over.

Phillip gasped and jerked back, but not in time to avoid the orange stream cascading into his lap.

"Oh dear." Tilley hopped up and reached for a towel.

Phillip muttered a curse as he swiped his napkin at his pants leg.

Surprise rippled through Jenn. She hadn't heard that kind of language for months.

Toby shrunk into his chair. "Sorry."

"It's all right, Toby." Jenn narrowed her eyes and sent Phillip a sharp glance. "It's just a little juice."

Tilley and Jenn tried to engage Phillip in conversation through the rest of breakfast, but his answers were brief and his irritation obvious. Jenn couldn't believe he would let a little accident spoil the meal. After they'd finished and cleared the table, Jenn turned to Phillip. "Well, I'm headed out to the gallery."

"Already?" He glanced at his watch, a disgruntled look settling over his features again.

She lifted her key ring from the hook by the refrigerator. "I need to turn on the air conditioner and cool things off before we open."

He cocked his head toward the mudroom, signaling that he wanted to speak to her alone.

She led the way out the back door and on to the porch. "What is it?"

"Darling, I understand you want to help your brother and his wife, but we need to make arrangements for our flight back to Oregon."

"I told you last night, I want to talk to Wes and Lauren first, and I want you to meet them."

"Of course. I'm looking forward to it. But I don't want you to miss the audition on Thursday, and I'm not sure how long we can wait to make our reservations."

Jenn smoothed her hand down her sleeve. "I'm not ready to make a decision. We'll just have to wait and see what happens."

He studied her for a moment, a perplexed look lining his face. "You've changed, Jenn."

A feeling of confidence rose in her heart, and she nodded. "You're right. I have."

∽

BILL CHECKED his watch and hustled up the sun-splashed front steps of Tipton Bible Church. As he pulled open the front door, the sound of the congregation singing a lively praise chorus greeted him and confirmed he was a few minutes late.

People were going to begin wondering about him. He'd missed church the day after the wedding because he'd driven Wes and Lauren to the airport. Last Sunday he'd been called to take part in the search for a little girl who had wandered away from her family's campsite near Mirror Lake. They found her a few hours later, and he was glad to help, but he wanted to be sure and touch base with Pastor Dan today to let him know where he'd been the past couple weeks.

Glancing into the sanctuary, he searched for a seat near the back then slipped inside as the song ended and everyone sat down.

Bill nodded to Howard Clarkson, Tipton's postmaster and owner of the general store. His old friend scooted down and made room for him at the end of the second pew from the back.

"Good to see you, Bill," Howard whispered. "Where've you been?"

Bill suppressed a chuckle as he settled into his seat. He supposed this was one of the advantages of attending a small church—people missed you when you were away. "I just got back from North Carolina on Friday."

Howard lifted his silver brows. "Visitin' your folks?"

Bill nodded. He wasn't ready to spread the news about the other reason for his trip, and if he told Howard, that's exactly what would happen.

The job offer from Hawk Mountain had come through yesterday. He'd thanked them and asked for a few more days to make a final decision. They'd been surprised by his request but agreed to give him until September first. He hoped six days was long enough to find out what Jenn planned to do.

He'd had a rough time sleeping the last two nights knowing Phillip was in town and Jenn was considering returning to Oregon with him. The decision about the new job also weighed heavily on his mind. Hopefully, he could fill in Wes and Lauren when he picked them up at the airport this afternoon. Maybe they could convince Jenn to send Phillip packing.

Pastor Dan opened his Bible and began reading Psalm Seventy-seven. As Bill listened, his gaze traveled around the sanctuary. He noticed Tilley sitting two rows in front of him. The woman next to Tilley turned and whispered something to her.

Bill's eyes widened as he caught sight of Jenn's familiar profile. Leaning slightly to the left, he spotted Phillip seated next to her and groaned under his breath. Charlotte Chambers, seated directly in front of Bill, lifted her fussy baby to her shoulder blocking his view. He scooted down the pew until his arm touched Howard's. The older man turned and raised his silver brows.

"Sorry," Bill whispered. "I was just trying to see who's sitting with Tilley."

Howard squinted and then looked back at Bill. "Why,

that's Wes's sister, Jennifer." His forehead creased as he sent Bill a confused look. "You brought her into the store and introduced her to me, remember?"

"Of course I remember," Bill whispered back. "I've just never seen her here before."

"Oh, she's been coming quite a while. At least three or four times, I'd say."

Bill's heartbeat kicked into high gear. "You sure about that?"

Arlene Clarkson tapped her husband on the thigh with her church bulletin. "The usher is going to ask you boys to step outside if you don't hush."

Bill nodded an apology and slid down to the end of the pew. He tried to focus on Pastor Dan, but his mind and eyes kept drifting back to Jenn.

Less than three minutes into the sermon Phillip draped his arm around Jenn's shoulder. A playful look filled his face as he leaned closer and whispered something in her ear.

Bill clenched his jaw and forced his gaze away. Jenn was here, and she was listening to a great sermon. That's all that mattered. But he had a hard time convincing himself that was true as he watched Phillip gently rub her shoulder and tickle her neck with a strand of her hair.

Twenty minutes later, Bill bowed his head and tried to concentrate on the words of the closing prayer. As soon as he heard "amen", he stood and grabbed his Bible from the pew. He glanced at Jenn and Phillip, debating if he should hightail it out of there or wait to speak to Jenn. Before he could decide, Julia stepped across the aisle.

"Hey, Bill. How was your trip?" A warm smile lit up her face as she greeted him.

"It was good." He swallowed and forced a half smile. He hadn't noticed Julia sitting over there.

"What time are you going to pick up Wes and Lauren?"

"Around five." He glanced to the right, checking on Jenn

and Phillip. They stood together in the center aisle by their pew. Tilley's hand rested on Jenn's arm as she introduced her to a friend.

"I can't wait to see them," Julia bit her lip and leaned closer. "I've got some news."

Bill focused on Julia again. "What kind of news?"

Her blue eyes twinkled. "I met someone."

Surprise rippled through him. "Really?"

She nodded. "He came into the office last week to list a house he inherited on Ingram Road. His name is Tanner Winslow. He's from New Jersey."

"Wow . . . that's great." Julia deserved someone special, but a question rose in his mind, and his smile faltered. "He's committed to the Lord, right?"

She rolled her eyes. "Of course. I wouldn't be interested in him if he wasn't."

How many times had he told himself the same thing? But his feelings for Jenn ran deep even though her faith seemed like a small, flickering flame. But being attracted to someone and even caring for them deeply didn't mean you were right for each other.

Frowning, he shook off his conflicting thoughts. He'd been praying for Jenn for months, they all had. Now she was coming to church consistently. That had to be a good sign. God must be working in her heart. If only he could talk to her and find out what she was thinking, but it didn't look like this was a good time. Phillip hovered next to her as she continued talking to Tilley and her friends.

"Bill?"

He turned back to Julia. "Sorry, I missed that."

"I said, I'd offer to go with you to pick up Wes and Lauren, but I've got to help my dad this afternoon."

His words caught in his throat as Jenn and Phillip walked up the aisle toward them. She looked amazing in a soft-green dress. But it wasn't her clothes that held his attention, it was the way her eyes lit up when she saw him.

A smile bloomed on her lips. "Hi, Bill."

He nodded and glanced away, his throat so tight he wasn't sure if he could speak.

Julia gave her a quick hug and sent a curious glance at Phillip. Jenn introduced him, only offering his name.

"I'm Jenn's fiancé from Oregon," Phillip added.

Julia's eyes widened for a split second, then she reached out and shook his hand. "I'm Julia Berkley. It's nice to meet you." As she stepped back, she shot Bill a questioning glance.

He gripped his Bible and glared at Phillip.

Tilley stepped into their circle. "Jenn, would you mind picking up Toby from his Sunday school class? I need to catch Martha Hopkins before she leaves."

"Okay." Jenn hesitated, her gaze darting from Phillip to Bill. "I'll be right back."

"I have to run, too," Julia said, taking Jenn's arm. "I've got an open house in West Harmon at one."

Jenn looked over her shoulder at Bill once more before she disappeared into the foyer.

Phillip rocked back on his heels, a smug smile lifting one side of his mouth. "I'd say it's good to see you again, but we're in church, so I shouldn't lie."

Bill shook his head. "You don't pull any punches do you?"

"Why should I? You deserve to know the truth."

"What?" He snorted. "That you don't like me?"

"No, that Jenn and I are leaving on Monday."

Bill clenched his fists. "I don't believe that."

"It doesn't matter what you believe. She's flying out with me tomorrow night."

"She said she'd talk to Wes and Lauren first."

"Of course." He lifted his brows. "We want to personally invite them to our wedding."

He grabbed hold of Phillip's arm. "I know you walked out

on Jenn after you saw her burns." Phillip tried to pull away, but Bill clamped on tighter. "You hurt her like that again, and you'll have to answer to me."

Phillip jerked his arm free. "That will be a little difficult since Jenn and I will be in Oregon and you'll be here . . . or will it be North Carolina?" He brushed the wrinkles on his shirtsleeve.

"It doesn't matter where I go. If Jenn needs me, she can call, and I'll be there."

"Well, don't hold your breath. She won't be calling."

"I'll be in touch with her. You can count on it. So don't think you can pull anything like that again."

Phillip's face darkened. "What happens between Jenn and me is none of your business. You have no claim on her."

The truth came crashing down on Bill like a crushing avalanche, pushing the air from his lungs.

Phillip was right. He couldn't protect Jenn no matter how much he wanted to.

"Give it up, Morgan." Phillip's smug smile returned. "She's marrying me."

He reeled back. This was his fault. He had forfeited his right to a relationship with Jenn when he decided not to talk about his faith or his feelings for her. That choice had cost him the woman that he loved. He struggled to pull in a breath, then turned and strode out of the church.

CHAPTER 24

Jenn clicked her seatbelt and scanned the church parking lot. Only a few vehicles remained, and Bill's truck wasn't one of them. Disappointment tugged at her heart. She'd hoped to find out if he'd accepted the job in North Carolina before she made her decision. It shouldn't matter. He'd made it clear he wasn't interested in a future with her. But for some reason she didn't feel right moving ahead without knowing his plans.

She glanced across at Phillip, and a queasy feeling hit her empty stomach. They planned to have lunch at the Green Mountain Café before they took a drive, but Jenn wasn't sure she'd be able to eat anything the way she felt now. She couldn't really blame Phillip. She was the one whose head and heart were pulling her in two different directions, tossing her poor stomach back and forth between them.

Mentally, she shook herself. She had to stop thinking about Bill and make an effort to connect with Phillip. He was the one who had traveled all the way across the country to find her and renew their relationship. "So how did you like the service?"

He started the car and cranked the air conditioning on full

blast. "They ought to cool things off in there if they expect people to come to services in the summer."

"It was pretty warm, but what did you think of pastor Dan's teaching?"

Phillip looked over his shoulder as he backed out of the parking space. "I had a hard time following him. I'm not sure what he was trying to say."

She sighed, barely able to hide her frustration. Why couldn't Phillip have at least tried to listen? His flirtatious teasing had embarrassed her and distracted everyone around them. When she realized Bill was sitting a few rows behind them, watching it all, she'd wanted to crawl under the pew and disappear.

Jenn forced her attention back to Phillip as he pulled out of the parking lot and sped down the winding two-lane road. They caught up with a slow-moving truck. Phillip muttered and swerved over the double yellow line to pass. A silver van approached in the oncoming lane.

"Look out!" Jenn gasped and gripped the edge of her seat as they hurtled past the truck and swerved into their lane just in time to avoid a collision with the van. "Would you please slow down?"

He shot her an irritated glance, but he eased back on the gas. Jenn released her death grip, but her stomach stayed in a tight knot.

Phillip's driving wasn't the only thing bothering her. Personality differences and character issues she'd never noticed before now seemed to stick out like noxious weeds in a lovely garden. How could he have changed so much in five months?

Closing her eyes, she lay back against the headrest. *Father, I'm not sure what to do. Please make it clear to me.*

Portions of the sermon floated through her mind, reminding her God would never leave her or forsake her . . . He would provide everything she truly needed . . . and He loved her with an everlasting love. A slow building sense of peace flowed through her, calming her heart and mind.

She was the one who had changed.

She was a different person than the grieving, scarred woman who had arrived on Bill's doorstep almost five months ago. Her scars hadn't faded, but they didn't hold the same power over her anymore.

Wonder filled her as that realization settled in her heart. How had it happened? The answer came swiftly, tightening her throat with emotion. Bill's friendship and acceptance had given her the courage to stop hiding her scars, and that had freed her to accept the changes in her life and her appearance. His caring example had helped her open her heart to God, and that was bringing the healing she'd longed for.

Memories of Bill's fierce response to Phillip and his warning against returning to Oregon with him rose in her mind, stirring up more doubts.

Opening her eyes, she turned to Phillip. A shiver traveled through her as she considered what she was about to say, but it was the only choice that made sense.

"Phillip?"

He turned to her.

"I've been doing a lot of thinking. I'm not comfortable with the idea of us living together, and I can't afford to get my own apartment, so I don't—"

Phillip reached across and took her hand. "Please, don't let a lack of money make this decision for you."

"I have to think about it. I have less than two-hundred dollars in my bank account."

He smiled and squeezed her hand. "That's all going to change very soon."

A warning flashed through her, and she slipped her hand out of his. "What do you mean?"

"I was going to wait until we got back to Oregon to talk to you about this." He sent her a sheepish grin.

Apprehension tightened her stomach as he pulled to the side of the road and turned off the car.

He shifted in his seat and faced her. "I met with a personal injury lawyer in Portland. He's been working on your case for a couple months. He's sure we can sue the construction company and win several hundred thousand, maybe even a million."

Her jaw dropped. "You talked to a lawyer without me?"

"I had to, darling. You weren't there, and you have to get moving on cases like this so you don't miss your window of opportunity."

Confusion swirled through her. "But I don't know if I want to sue someone."

"Of course you do." He reached for her hand again and wrapped his fingers tightly around hers. "Don't worry. It's not like you're suing an individual. No one is going to go bankrupt or anything like that. It's a business. They have insurance to cover this kind of thing. You'd just be getting what you deserve." His eyes glowed with excitement. "Think of it, Jenn. We could buy a house, travel, do whatever we want. We'd be set for life." Cocking his head, he lifted one brow. "Maybe we could even start our own theater company."

She grimaced and pulled her hand away. "With my money."

"Yes, of course it's your money, darling." A worried frown creased his forehead.

"But if we get married, it would be your money too, right?"

"Well . . . yes. Everything I have would be yours, and whatever you have would be mine." He released a nervous chuckle. "That's the way it works when you're married. You combine all your assets."

She shook her head. "I'm not comfortable with that."

He pulled back, scowling. "With what? Sharing everything with me?"

"No, with going to court and suing the construction company."

He let loose an exasperated huff. "Jenn, you lost everything you owned. You suffered tremendously. Someone should pay for that."

"How would you know?" She leveled her cool gaze at him. "You weren't there."

A hint of panic flickered in his eyes, but he quickly doused it and leaned toward her. "I saw your burns the night of the fire, Jenn. They're . . . extensive. The lawyer said we could sue for disfigurement, pain, suffering, loss of wages, and maybe more."

A hot irritation surged through her. Who did he think he was, contacting a lawyer and making those kinds of decisions for her? She lifted her chin. "What if I won't sue them?"

"But this is our chance to get everything we've ever wanted. You can't throw it all away!"

The sick feeling in her stomach rose and burned her throat. It was all clear to her now. He'd searched for her because of the money.

"I've never believed being rich guarantees happiness." Conviction flowed through her, strengthening her words. "And it won't help at all if you're married to the wrong person."

His face darkened. "Are you saying you don't want to marry me?"

A shiver raced up her back. She would not be intimidated by him or anyone else. Raising her chin, she met the challenge in his eyes. "Yes, that's what I'm saying."

"But getting married was your idea," he insisted.

"That was before . . . other things are more important to me now."

He scowled at her. "Like what?"

"Like having a life that has meaning and purpose."

"And how do you intend to find that?" His mocking tone grated on her.

She didn't know if he really wanted an explanation, but she sent off a quick prayer, asking he would at least try to understand. "For a long time I was angry with God for all the painful things that happened to me. I thought saying I didn't believe in Him would somehow keep anything else bad from happening. But that only made me more miserable, because deep inside I knew He existed, and He wanted me to come back to Him."

Phillip shook his head. "What has that got to do with a meaningful life?"

She groaned inwardly but pressed on determined to try her best to make it clear. Maybe God would use her to help Phillip see how important faith could be in his life.

"I've met people here who've shown me how to know God in a personal way and how to grow stronger in my faith. That's important to me. And that's what I want, even more than a lot of money, or marriage, or a lead role in a play, or anything else."

He shook his head, looking confused. "Okay, but can't you pursue that in Portland? There are churches all over town. I'm sure you could find one you'd like."

"I'm not just talking about going to church, I'm talking about a relationship with Jesus. And in order for that relationship to grow, I need to be in a place where people understand that and where I have the love and support I need. I have that here, Phillip."

"So, this is it? After all I've done for you, you're just giving up on us?"

She studied the angry tilt of his chin, the haughty lift of his brows. He didn't get it, and she wasn't sure he ever would. But that wasn't the only issue between them. "You know, not once this weekend have you said you loved me."

He pulled back. "But I came all the way out here. If that doesn't prove I love you, then I don't know what will."

"Okay." She unhooked her seatbelt and slipped off the lacy white shirt she had worn over her sleeveless sundress. Cool determination flowed through her as she turned over her arm, giving him full view of her scars.

He pulled back, his lips twisting into a painful grimace. "Oh, Jenn . . . that's exactly why we should sue the construction company for all they're worth."

She held her arm steady. "It goes all the way up my neck and across in front. I'll look like this for the rest of my life, Phillip. It's not changing."

He shook his head, his face pale. "There's got to be plastic surgery or something they can do to fix it."

His reaction sealed her choice. She pulled her arm back and laid it in her lap. Raising her chin, she looked him in the eyes. "Take me home."

∼

Bill shoved the front door closed behind him and trudged through the quiet house. With a weary shake of his head, he laid his Bible on the counter and glanced around the empty kitchen.

The afternoon sun shone through the sliding glass door spreading light across the room, but it couldn't penetrate the gloom hovering over him. Sinking into a chair, he lowered his head into his hands.

Father, how could You let this happen? I was so sure You were going to answer my prayers. Now it doesn't matter if I stay in Vermont or move to North Carolina. Jenn's leaving, and I'm losing her forever to that, that—

Bill clenched his jaw and pushed himself out of the chair. Praying wouldn't help. It was over. Done. He had to get a get a hold of himself and forget about Jennifer Evans.

Yeah, right. Like that was going to happen any time soon.

He wasn't hungry, but he opened the cabinet and searched the shelves. Nothing looked good. Finally, he pulled out the bag of rice and set it on the counter. Maybe he'd feel more like eating after the rice simmered for a while.

He grabbed a pot from the lower cabinet and kicked the cabinet door closed. The loud bang startled him. He had to stop acting like an idiot. So, things hadn't worked out with Jenn. He'd get over it. Maybe not in the near future, but eventually. Like maybe in five or ten years.

Stifling a groan, he dumped rice in a measuring cup. Some spilled over the top. He swiped it aside, and his hand skidded through a sticky spot of day-old jam on the counter. Grumbling, he rinsed off his hand and filled the pot with water. With his fingers still dripping, he turned on the front burner and centered the pan over the flames.

Where were Phillip and Jenn eating lunch? He grabbed a kitchen towel and dried his hands as he mulled it over. Probably at some ritzy restaurant in Rutland. He could picture them now seated side-by-side in a plush booth with dim lighting. Phillip would slip his arm around her shoulder and whisper in her ear. She would smile and lean closer, inviting his kiss.

Bill's stomach convulsed, and a fierce growl exploded from his throat. He slammed the upper cabinet and threw the towel across the counter. Without a backward glance, he stormed out the sliding glass door and down the back steps.

Stomping through the tall grass and muttering under his breath, he followed the trail downhill, toward the rushing stream. The trees closed in overhead, shading the rugged path. He continued on, beating his way through the forest, not caring where he ended up.

Less than five minutes into his trek, he tripped over a fallen limb and crashed to the ground. Air whooshed out of his lungs, and gravel bit into his chin and hands. A curse flew from his lips. Immediately, a piercing shard of regret cut through him.

Oh, God, forgive me. But it hurts so much. I don't want to lose Jenn. Waves of sorrow broke over him, and hot tears burned his eyes.

Give it up, Bill. Give it to Me. I know what's best.

He rolled over and sat up, wrestling against the gentle voice in his soul. Closing his eyes, he slowed his breathing and tried to focus his churning thoughts.

Bittersweet memories of times he'd spent with Jenn rose in his mind. Why hadn't he tried harder to explain the importance of his faith? Why hadn't he found a way to make her understand? He'd prayed for her so many times! Why hadn't God answered?

A sudden realization hit him. Almost every prayer was motivated by a desire that she would come back to God, not so much for her sake, but so that they could be together.

His selfishness slapped him in the face, and remorse swept through him. Oh, God, I'm so sorry. That's not the kind of love she deserves. Please draw her closer to You even though she's leaving. Pain twisted through him, but he pushed it aside. You know I love her, but I surrender all my desires and hopes to You. Watch over her and protect her. Give her the life and love she deserves.

He rose to his feet and lifted his eyes to the leafy canopy. His heart still felt heavy, but knowing he'd surrendered everything to God gave him a measure of peace.

The sudden gust of wind blew through the trees carrying a faint smell of smoke. Frowning, he turned and sniffed the air.

CHAPTER 25

Jenn pulled open the screen and walked through the back door at Long Meadow. The delicious scent of something baking in the kitchen drifted toward her and made her stomach growl. Was it Tilley's famous cinnamon rolls or her delicious oatmeal raisin cookies? Jenn couldn't tell, but either one sounded good.

"Is that you, Jenn?" Tilley called.

"Yes, it's me." She rounded the corner and walked into the cozy kitchen. A tray of raisin-studded cookies cooled on a metal rack near the stove. Their tempting cinnamon scent drew her closer.

Tilley stood at the counter stirring a tall glass pitcher of iced tea. "I didn't expect you back until this evening." She looked past Jenn's shoulder. "Where's Phillip?"

Jenn took a warm cookie from the tray. "He went back to the bed and breakfast."

Tilley's spoon stilled and she looked up. "Is everything all right?"

"I won't be going back to Oregon with him."

Tilley dropped the spoon into the iced tea. "Hallelujah! She's seen the light!"

Jenn laughed and almost choked on her cookie.

The older woman reached over and patted her on the back. "Sorry, dear. Are you okay?"

Jenn coughed and nodded. "Why didn't you tell me how you felt?"

"I was planning to, but I decided to pray and give the Lord a chance to take care of things first."

"Thanks for praying. The answer came through loud and clear today."

"I'm glad to hear it. I wasn't too impressed with that young man, but even more than that, I couldn't bear the thought of you leaving us and moving so far away."

"Neither could I." Jenn gave Tilley a hug and headed upstairs to change.

She slipped out of her dress and laid it on the bed. As she turned and reached to open her dresser drawer, she glanced at the scars on her right arm. Slowly she turned her arm toward the light streaming in the window and examined the familiar pattern of mottled and twisted skin.

A sense of wonder swept through her. God had taken something she considered painful and ugly and used it to expose Phillip's motive and protect her from making a choice she would regret. Her scars had been transformed and their meaning changed forever. Gratitude flooded her heart, and she whispered her thanks to God.

As she came down the stairs a few minutes later, the phone rang. "I'll get it," she called and picked up the receiver. "Hello."

"This is Harriet Walker, Bill Morgan's neighbor. Is Bill there?" The elderly woman's voice sounded strained and shaky.

Jenn frowned. Why was she looking for Bill? "No, he's not here. I saw him at church earlier, but I'm not sure where he went this afternoon."

"Oh, dear."

Apprehension rippled through Jenn. "Is everything okay?"

"Well, I'm not sure. It's probably nothing, but I thought I saw some smoke by Bill's house."

"Smoke?" Jenn gripped the phone more tightly.

"I called over there, but no one answered."

Jenn's pulse raced, and her hands began to tremble. Where was Bill? Could he be he trapped inside his house, overcome by heat and smoke? No! That couldn't be true. She squeezed her eyes shut and forced those terrifying thoughts away.

"I'd go check myself," Harriet continued, "but I had surgery a few weeks ago, and I can't walk without—"

"That's okay. I'll go over there now. Thanks for calling." She hung up and ran into the kitchen. She found Tilley sitting at the table reading the Sunday paper.

"What's wrong, dear?" Concern lined Tilley's face.

Jenn explained Harriet's call. "I'm sure Bill's okay, but I want to drive over and check." She willed confidence into her voice, but it didn't stop her legs from feeling like jelly.

Tilley got up and reached for the phone. "We should call the fire department just in case."

"Good idea." Jenn snatched her purse off the counter and grabbed Wes's keys from the hook. When she reached the doorway, she stopped and looked over her shoulder. "Would you pray for Bill?" She had to swallow before she could speak again. "I couldn't bear it if something happened to him."

"Of course, dear. I'm sure he's fine, but I'll pray for you both." Tilley sent her a reassuring smile. "Now go on. The sooner you see him, the better you'll feel."

"Thanks." Jenn hurried out the back door.

Tilley was right. There was no need to panic. Bill was okay. But shivers raced up her back, and she couldn't stop the feeling of dread building in her stomach. She hopped in Wes's car and sent gravel flying as she took off.

She made the drive to Bill's in less than four minutes.

Careening around the corner onto Shelton Road, she continued her prayer, "Please, God, don't let anything happen to Bill."

Leaning forward, she scanned the sky, looking for any sign of smoke, but trees on both sides of the road blocked her view. She rounded the curve and screeched to a stop in front of Bill's house. Peering out the window, her heart clenched. Smoke curled out from under the eaves on the left side of the house. Bill's black truck sat in the driveway. She shoved her car into park and sprang out the driver's door.

The blaring wail of the smoke alarm from inside sent a chilling tremor through her. She ran toward the house and dashed around the side following the smoke. What she saw there stopped her cold. Flames licked up the outside, melting the siding and blackening wood around the open kitchen window.

She screamed Bill's name and tore around back. With her heart pounding in her ears, she flew up the stairs and across the deck. Her hand froze on the metal handle as she stared through the sliding glass door. A churning cloud of smoke swirled through the living room, and greedy flames leaped up the kitchen wall around the window above the sink.

Bill couldn't be in there. He couldn't be.

But what if he was?

She shoved the door open, and noxious smoke billowed out around her. Squeezing her eyes against the stinging pain, she called Bill's name. The only answer was the crackling flames sucking in the new surge of oxygen from the open door and the wailing alarm.

Terrifying images of stumbling through her flaming apartment filled her mind. Searing pain scorched her arms again as it had five months ago.

How could she go in there? How could she face the flames again? Fear gripped her by the throat, and blinding panic swirled through her. Oh, God, help me. I can't do this. I can't!

But she had to. Love demanded it, even it if meant walking through the fire to find him. Gathering her courage, she stepped inside on trembling legs and pulled the door closed behind her. Crouching low, she slipped along the central wall toward the bedroom opposite the kitchen. She ducked through the doorway and quickly searched the bedroom and bathroom. Then, holding her breath, she ran back past the flaming kitchen, through the living room, and out the sliding glass door.

Coughing and gasping for air, she leaned on the deck rail and tried to focus her racing thoughts.

If Bill wasn't in those rooms, the only other option was upstairs. But wouldn't he have come down when he heard the alarm? She rubbed her stinging eyes, trying to make sense of the situation. What if the fire had started upstairs, and the smoke was so thick he'd passed out? If that was true, how could she survive going up there to look for him?

Oh, God, please show me what to do. She turned and peered through the glass again. Flames shot up the kitchen wall and licked across the ceiling. How much time did she have before the fire burned through and consumed the rooms above? Five minutes? Ten? She had no idea. Only one thing was clear—If she didn't go now, it would be too late to find Bill and get him out.

She pulled the door open and dashed back into the heat and smoke. Holding her breath again, she ran across the living room, opened the door to the stairwell and fled up the stairs calling Bill's name.

Her frantic search took less than thirty seconds. She stood in the hall, dazed and confused as the smoke drifted up through the heat vents and thickened the air. Her throat felt raw from coughing, and her eyes burned with tears. *Oh God, where is he? I have to find him.*

Dizziness made her head spin. She reached for the wall and sank down at the top of the stairs.

~

Bill hiked along the trail by the stream, a vague sense of urgency pushing him along. A distant siren echoed across the valley. He stopped and sniffed the air. The smoke he'd smelled earlier had disappeared, or the wind had shifted. It probably wasn't anything serious. There hadn't been a fire in Tipton for years.

But an uneasy feeling lifted the hairs on the back of his neck as the siren grew louder. He took the shortcut through his neighbor's property, climbed the hill, and came out on Shelton road about fifty yards from his house.

Someone called his name, and he looked up. Harriet Walker stood on her porch, waving to him. He smiled and lifted his hand, but she continued to wave, motioning him closer. He jogged over to her front yard.

"Look at all that smoke." Her hand trembled as she pointed past the trees surrounding his yard. "I'm afraid it's your house."

Adrenalin shot through Bill. He spun away and ran down the road. The side of his house came into view first, and he skidded to a stop, a rush of dread twisting through him.

Smoke billowed out the kitchen window, and scorching flames leaped up the outside wall. He ran around front. Wes's car sat in the driveway parked at an odd angle with the driver's door hanging open.

Terror flooded him. He spun in a circle, searching for Jenn, praying he'd see her standing in one of the neighbors' yards. She wasn't there. A second surge of panic hit him full force.

He yelled her name and rushed toward the front door. A warning flashed through his mind. Go around back. He jumped from the porch and ran around the other side of the house. No flames were visible there, but smoke hung in the trees like an eerie veil.

He dashed up the steps and ran across the deck to the

sliding glass door. For a split second he hesitated, debating if he should wait for the firemen. One glance at the swirling smoke beyond the glass, and he made up his mind. If Jenn was in there, he had to get her out now.

Pulling up his shirttail to cover his mouth and nose, he opened the door. Scorching heat rushed out at him.

Oh, Father, help me. Dropping to his knees, he crawled into the house. Smoke singed his nose and throat. Sweat poured down his face and dripped into his eyes. The fire hissed and crackled as it engulfed the cabinets over the stove. He'd never get past the kitchen to check the downstairs bedroom or bathroom. He turned and crawled through the living room toward the door leading upstairs.

A faint cough sounded beyond the door. He jumped up and flung it open then squinted into the smoky stairwell.

"Bill!" Jenn stumbled down the stairs.

He grabbed her, a mixture of panic and relief shooting through him. "Come on." He wrapped his arm around her and pulled her to his side. They crouched down and wove their way through the living room. Only a few steps from the sliding glass door, he looked back and spotted his laptop on the table. It held all his files for work, including the grant applications he'd spent weeks preparing. "Go outside. I'm gonna' get my laptop."

"No!" She grabbed his arm.

"I'll be okay." He pushed her toward the door and dashed back toward the flaming kitchen. With a swift jerk, he pulled the laptop's power cord from the wall.

Jenn screamed.

He looked up. A burning hunk of the ceiling broke loose. Fireworks exploded in his head, and he crashed to the floor.

~

Energy surged through Jenn like a shock of high voltage electricity. She ran to Bill and kicked the smoldering wood off his back. Sparks flew up and singed her legs. She dropped to her knees and brushed the burning embers off his scorched shirt with her bare hands.

"Bill!" She grabbed his shoulder, but he didn't move. Panic welled in her throat. "Oh, God, please help me."

Before she finished her prayer, a plan formed in her mind. She shoved the smoking wood out of the way with her foot then rolled him over. Reaching under his arms, she summoned strength she didn't know she had and dragged him out the door and across the deck.

Kneeling beside him, she searched his soot-smeared face. "Bill?" She laid her trembling hand on his chest and leaned closer. His breath brushed her cheek, and relief poured through her.

She lifted her head and listened as the fire truck rolled to a stop out front and the firemen began shouting orders to each other.

"Thank you, Lord. Thank you." Her eyes slid closed, and tears rolled down her cheeks. "Please help them get the fire under control. And Bill has to be okay, please. He loves You Lord. I know he does. If it wasn't for him, I never would've—"

A hand gripped her arm, and her eyes flew open.

"You're praying for me?" Bill whispered, his voice ragged with emotion.

She nodded and smiled through her tears then brushed the hair off his forehead. "Of course I am."

A look of amazement and love filled his glistening eyes. He slowly sat up and reached for her, pulling her in for a tight hug. "Thank you, God," he choked out. "Thank you so much."

She clung to him, adding her silent prayer to his, her heart full and overflowing with love and gratefulness.

CHAPTER 26

*J*enn turned in the driveway as the sun dipped behind the roof of the house. She glanced across the front seat at Bill, and her heart warmed. Soot lined his tired face, but he looked wonderful to her.

He pointed down the long gravel drive. "Look, there's Wes and Lauren."

Wes lifted a large suitcase from the trunk of Tilley's car, and Toby reached to help him. Tilley handed Lauren a shopping bag from the back seat. They all looked up as Jenn pulled in and parked next to them.

Lauren dropped her bag and hurried over to open Jenn's door. Leaning down, she looked in. "Are you okay? Tilley told us about the fire."

They had called Tilley from Bill's cell phone while the firemen fought the blaze and then again from the emergency room at the hospital to give an update and ask her to pick up Wes and Lauren at the airport.

"We're fine." Jenn stepped out and gave Lauren a tight hug. "They thought Bill had a concussion, but he had a CT scan, and the doctors say everything looks okay. We just need to keep an eye on him tonight."

Wes abandoned his suitcase on the driveway and walked over to greet Bill as he climbed out of the car. "Hey, brother." He slapped him on the back and pulled him in for a bear hug. "I'm sorry about your house." He stepped back and looked him over. "Man, you look beat."

"Yeah, we both are." Bill glanced at Jenn, concern in his eyes.

"So how bad is the house?" Wes asked.

"The kitchen is destroyed, and there's smoke and water damage in most of the other rooms. It'll take a while to make all the repairs. But we're okay. That's what matters." He sent Jenn a weary smile, and her heart melted.

"You're staying here in the meantime," Wes said, "and you can count on us to help with those repairs."

"Thanks."

Tilley fluttered around passing out hugs as they gathered up the suitcases and moved toward the house. Toby darted back and forth between Bill and Jenn, begging to know more about the fire.

Lauren laid her hand on his shoulder. "Toby, give them a chance to catch their breath. I'm sure they want to come in and get cleaned up before they tell us about it."

Jenn sent Lauren a grateful smile.

Tilley and Lauren prepared a quick supper of chicken salad sandwiches, juicy sliced tomatoes, and cold watermelon while Bill and Jenn took quick showers and changed into clean clothes. They joined everyone in the kitchen and took turns recounting all that had happened. When the food was ready, they carried their plates outside and settled on the back patio.

Jenn ate a few bites of her sandwich and a little watermelon, then she set aside her plate and listened to Bill finish telling everyone about their trip to the emergency room and the drive back to see his damaged house.

"It's a miracle neither of you were seriously hurt." Tilley stood and passed the plate of oatmeal raisin cookies.

Bill accepted a cookie. "God was definitely watching out for us today."

Lauren nodded. "You're right about that." She and Wes sat on the wicker love seat opposite Jenn and Bill, their hands clasped as they watched Toby toss a small red ball across the grass for Bryn, Tilley's Border collie. Little Sophie scampered after Bryn, her tongue hanging out the side of her mouth.

The sky faded from bright magenta and burnt orange to soft pink and purple. Cicadas buzzed in the trees, and crickets serenaded them from the garden.

Jenn sighed and laid her head back on the pillow of her wicker chair. She glanced around at each face, and gratefulness welled up in her heart. This was her family, each one so special to her. What an amazing gift she'd been given.

Her gaze settled on Bill. He sat in the chair next to her wearing a clean blue t-shirt and brown cargo shorts he'd borrowed from Wes. When he washed up, he'd missed a small soot smudge along his jaw. She felt temped to reach over and wipe it away, but she lifted her glass of iced tea and took a drink instead.

Bill leaned closer. His arm brushed hers as he reached for another cookie. He took a bite and winked at her.

She felt a blush steal into her cheeks as she returned his smile, sending him a private message she hoped he understood.

"Ahh, this is the life." Wes put his feet up and slipped his arm around his new wife.

A happy, teasing light shone in Lauren's eyes. "Well don't get too comfortable. It's almost time to go in and put Toby to bed."

"Sounds good to me. I'm looking forward to it. I haven't tucked him in for two weeks." Wes shifted his gaze to Jenn. "But first, there's something I need to ask my sister."

"What?" Jenn sat up a little straighter.

"Tilley said you've been going to church with her the last three weeks." He lifted his brows. "So, what's going on?"

Lauren groaned. "Wes, give the girl a break."

Bill shot Jenn a worried glance.

"It's okay." Jenn focused on Wes again. "I know it must seem strange to you after everything I've said, but I've been reading the Bible Lauren gave me, and doing a lot of thinking."

"Come to any conclusions?" Wes tried to sound casual, but she could see how important this was to him.

"Yes . . ." She looked around the group, each one watching her expectantly. "I decided life is too short to stay stuck and miserable. I may never understand everything that's happened to me, but I'm learning God is in the business of healing and helping. That's what I need, so I'm asking Him to do that for me."

Wes's eyes widened and he raised his fist in the air. "Yes!"

Bill watched her with a proud smile and shining eyes.

"Thank you, Jesus." Lauren reached over and squeezed Jenn's hand. "I'm happy for you, Jenn. I know God has some very special plans for you."

"And speaking of plans . . ." Wes leaned forward. "What happened to the guy who showed up out of the blue telling everyone you were still engaged?"

"She sent that rat back to his hole," Bill muttered, a triumphant gleam in his eyes.

Jenn smiled, remembering Bill's indignant cry at the hospital when she'd told him Phillip had consulted a lawyer and hoped to win a huge settlement by suing the construction company for her injuries. Two nurses had pushed back the curtain and scurried in to find out what was wrong, followed by a doctor and a security guard.

"Phillip is probably on his way back to Portland by now," Jenn said.

Wes chuckled, and Lauren nudged him with her shoulder.

"You're not upset that he left?"

"No, I'm relieved actually. Our lives are going in different directions now. It never would've worked out."

"It's a good thing you realized that now," Lauren added. "Marriage is wonderful, but you need to find someone who shares your goals and values and truly loves you."

"That's very good advice, dear." Tilley stood and brushed the crumbs off her skirt. "Well, I think it's time for me to go inside." She began gathering up the dishes.

"I'll help you," Jenn offered.

Tilley waved her off. "I'm fine, dear. Why don't you and Bill stay out here and enjoy the evening." She lifted her silver brows and sent Lauren and Wes a meaningful look.

"That's our cue." Wes stood and held out his hand to Lauren.

She took it and rose to her feet. "Come on, Toby," she called. "Time to go in."

He tossed the ball for Sophie once more. "Aw, do we have to?"

Wes checked his watch. "We've got time for a story if you hustle."

Toby plucked up the ball and ran toward them. Wes scooped him up and tickled his ribs. Toby giggled and squirmed, but when Wes put him down, he raised his arms and asked him to do it again. Wes lifted him onto his shoulders, and they walked toward the house.

Bill smiled as he watched them go. "They make a great family."

"Yes, they do." Jenn settled back and released a deep sigh.

He reached across and took her hand. "You look happy."

"I am."

"Tell me why." He rubbed his thumb over the top of her hand, sending delightful tingles up her arm.

She bit her lip, wondering how much to share. They

hadn't really talked about their feelings for each other, though the events of the last few hours seemed to have taken them to a deeper level.

"I have a lot to be thankful for," she said softly.

"Such as?"

"Well . . . we're here together sharing this beautiful evening."

A tender look filled his eyes, whisking away her fears.

"I could've been on a plane tonight with Phillip, making the biggest mistake of my life."

"I'm glad you didn't go." He hesitated a few seconds, looking like he wanted to say more. "Do you want to take a walk?"

"That would be nice." He took her hand again and they strolled across the yard, past the barn. Lightning bugs danced through the bushes at the edge of the meadow like little fairy lights.

Bill clasped her hand more tightly and cleared his throat. "They offered me the job at Hawk Mountain."

His words snatched away her breath.

"But I'm going to turn it down," he added.

Jenn gasped and spun toward him. "Really?"

"Yep." He grinned, obviously enjoying her response. "If you're staying, I'm staying."

She laughed, relief pouring through her. "Why did it take us so long to figure that out?"

His smile faded and he grew more sober. "I knew how I felt about you all along, but I didn't want to get in the way of what the Lord was doing in your heart."

"How could you staying here get in the way?"

"It's hard to explain." He gazed past her shoulder for a few seconds, the struggle evident on his face, then he looked in her eyes again. "I wanted us to be together, but I wasn't sure if it was going to work out because of all the faith issues you were struggling with, so leaving seemed like the only answer."

His words sank in and heaviness settled over her heart. They'd come very close to losing each other, and she hadn't understood the real issues separating them. "I wish you would've told me how you felt."

"Yeah. I'm sorry I didn't explain." He rubbed his hand down his face, tired lines creasing his forehead. "I've never been very good at talking about how I feel and what I believe, especially with someone I really care about." His eyes clouded with regret. "I'm sorry, Jenn. We probably could've avoided a whole lot of trouble if I'd told you straight out how much my faith means to me."

She thought about that for a moment, remembering all that had happened between them, then she looked up at him and smiled. "You did something better than that."

"What do you mean?"

"You showed me what faith looks like, how God loves me and accepts me just as I am. That means more to me than a hundred explanations ever could."

He shook his head and looked away.

"Don't you see? You lived what you believed every day, and God used that to touch my heart and helped me see He was real."

His Adam's apple bobbed, and when he looked back, his eyes glistened. "I don't see how I—"

She took his hands in hers. "Lots of people have talked to me about God, but I needed someone to show me what faith means, and that's what you did for me."

"That's just . . . wow, I don't know what to say."

Jenn laughed. "That's okay. You don't have to say anything. I'll show you what I mean." She stood on her tiptoes, slipped her arms around his neck and kissed him, gently at first, then more deeply with all the love overflowing from her heart. He responded with a passion that equaled hers.

"I love you, Jenn," he whispered, his voice husky and full of emotion. "So much."

Her smile deepened as she looked into his eyes. "Now you're talking."

He chuckled and pulled her closer. Their lips met again, and his kiss sent an undeniable message of love straight to her heart.

THE END

Dear Reader,

I hope you enjoyed your trip to Tipton, Vermont, and getting to know Jenn and Bill in SURRENDERED HEARTS. Jenn's journey of faith and healing is very dear to my heart. Every woman longs to know she is beautiful and loved. But pain from our past can make it difficult to see things clearly. It's a wonderful blessing when God demonstrates His love toward us through friends and family and then confirms those truths in His Word, the Bible.

My prayer for you, dear reader, is that you too will reach out to God and find the faith and love you have been looking for. He is always there waiting for you with His arms open wide!

I love to hear from my readers. Please feel free to email me at: carrie@turansky.com

Until next time ~ Happy Reading,
Carrie

Have you read ALONG CAME LOVE, Book One in the Vermont Blessings Series? It's available in print and eBook at Amazon.

Are you looking for another heartwarming contemporary romance series to enjoy? I've included the first chapter of SEEKING HIS LOVE, Book One in the Bayside Treasures Series. These three books are set in Fairhaven, Washington, the historic section of Bellingham. They feature a fun group of senior-aged women who are matchmakers for the younger generation. Each book as unique heroes and heroines. I hope you'll read on for a taste of life and love in Fairhaven!

~

SEEKING HIS LOVE
Book One in the Bayside Treasures Series

A SHIVER of anticipation raced up Rachel Clark's back as she stepped into the dark auditorium of the old Fairhaven Elementary School. Cool air ushered a dusty smell toward her, teasing her nose. With only the dim glow of the Exit signs to light her path, she made her way down the sloping aisle toward the stage.

The house lights came up. She blinked as her eyes adjusted to the sudden brightness, and then took in the scene. Rows of padded folding seats in three sections filled the cavernous hall. Two carpeted aisles led to a large proscenium stage with a wide, bow-shaped apron and a plush burgundy curtain.

Warmth and wonder tingled through her. "This is perfect." She turned and searched for Hannah Bodine.

The silver-haired curator of the local historical museum poked her head out from the sound booth at the back. Dressed in a flowing tropical-print blouse and coral Capri pants, she stepped into the aisle. "Do you like it?"

"Yes, it's exactly what we're looking for." Rachel hurried forward and mounted the steps. Waltzing to the middle of the stage, she scanned the auditorium. "Do you know how many seats there are?"

"Let's see." Hannah strolled forward, counting the rows of burgundy chairs. "Looks like almost four hundred."

Rachel smiled and nodded. "That's a hundred more than we have now." With a larger house they could increase their ticket sales and income, something she and her small staff desperately needed if they were going to hold on to their jobs.

"I think this would be a good home for your group," Hannah added. "Why don't I take you to meet Cameron McKenna, and you can make arrangements to speak to everyone at the co-op meeting tonight."

"That would be great." Rachel ran her hand along the velvet curtain as she crossed the stage, memories of past performances making her smile. She descended the wooden steps and met her friend down in front.

"Thanks, Hannah. This is really an answer to prayer. I was beginning to think we were going to be a homeless theater company." Rachel crossed her arms and rubbed away a chill brought on by that thought.

"It works out well for all of us. The school district is raising our rent." Hannah sighed and shook her head as she led the way up the aisle. "You'd think they'd be happy to receive any income from this old building. It sat empty for two years before we got together to rent it. We've made a lot of improvements, but if we want to hold on to it, we have to rent the remaining space."

Rachel nodded. It sounded like the Fairhaven Artist's Co-op needed her as much as she needed them. She blew out a deep breath and tried to relax her tense shoulders. This would work. It had to.

Finding the position as director of Northcoast Christian Youth Theater had been a miracle. She didn't want to think about disbanding and looking for another job. Returning to teaching wasn't an option, not after everything that had happened. She pushed those painful memories away and followed Hannah into the main hallway.

"That's Cam's frame shop." Hannah motioned toward the open door across the hall. "He handles all the finances for the co-op. He can give you the particulars about renting with us."

Rachel stepped forward, eager to meet him and discuss the details.

Hannah held out her hand to slow her down. "Cam might be a bit resistant to the idea. He's a little . . ." She bit her lip and glanced toward the ceiling. "Well, I suppose I should let you make up your own mind. Just be patient with him, dear."

Rachel smiled and nodded, certain she'd have no trouble winning him over. Persuasion was her middle name. Her exasperated mother used to say she could sell a dozen umbrellas to a desert nomad with no trouble at all.

She entered the shop where framed prints, photos, and original artwork lined the walls. Rows of mat and frame samples hung in a neat display on the back wall.

A tall man with broad shoulders and blond curly hair leaned over a workbench at the rear of the shop. He held a pair of needle nose pliers in his hand. The muscles on his forearm rippled as he twisted a sturdy wire to create a hanger across the back of a large frame lying facedown on the workbench. He looked up, and his piercing blue gaze connected with hers.

A shiver of awareness traveled through her. She straightened and returned his steady gaze. He looked about thirty-five with a strong chin and Roman nose. No doubt he'd be handsome if he didn't wear such a scowl.

"Good morning, Cam." Hannah crossed to the workbench and Rachel followed.

"Morning." He nodded to Hannah.

"This is Rachel Clark. She's interested in renting space with us."

His eyes lit up, and his scowl softened. "What kind of artwork do you do?"

"I'm the director of a theater group. We're interested in renting the auditorium, two classrooms, and an office."

"That's a lot of space." He laid aside the pliers. "Is this a new group, or are you already established?

"We're about four years old." Uneasiness prickled through her. She'd only been working as the director since the beginning of March, a little over two months. But she had six years of teaching high school drama and three summers with NCYT as the assistant director. So she wasn't stretching the truth too far when she included herself in that four year history. She could always explain later if he asked.

He looked her over more carefully. "Where are you meeting now?"

"We use Grace Community Church in North Bellingham, but they're opening a preschool, so we need to be out by the end of the month."

Recognition flickered in his eyes. "Is Sheldon James the pastor there?"

"Yes. Do you know him?"

"We're old friends."

She smiled at that good news. "He and the church have been very supportive."

"Sounds like Sheldon. He's a good man." He wiped his hand on a cloth. "So what kind of shows do you do?"

"They're all musicals. Our last two were *Annie* and *Oklahoma*. This summer we're doing *Anne of Green Gables*."

He continued to appraise her with his sharp gaze. "What do you call yourselves?"

She hesitated a split second, sending off a silent prayer. "Northcoast Christian Youth Theater."

He eyes widened, and a stormy expression broke over his face. "Youth? As in children?"

She lifted her chin. "Yes. Our students are ten to eighteen.

We hold after school drama classes September to May, and morning drama camps in the summer, along with afternoon and evening rehearsals for our musicals."

He gave a swift shake of his head. "That would never work here."

A shot of panic skittered along her nerves. "But you have the space. And from what Hannah said, you need to rent it."

He sent a disapproving glance at Hannah, then turned back to Rachel. "We're serious artists. Our shops are filled with expensive pieces. We can't have kids running all over the building."

Heat flashed into Rachel's face. "I can assure you my students are well-supervised."

"Sorry. I can't take that risk."

Rachel pulled in a calming breath. "I'm sure when you learn more about our program, you'll see how valuable we are to the community."

"It may be a good program, but it would be a bad idea to bring it here."

Hannah laid her hand on the workbench. "Cam, my granddaughter attends the summer camp and has been in two shows. I've seen the performances. They're a wonderful group of kids."

Rachel sent Hannah a grateful smile, then focused on Cam again. "Renting to us would bring in more customers."

He huffed. "The kids are going to buy artwork?"

"No, but their parents bring them to classes and rehearsals, and that would be the perfect opportunity for them to visit the shops and galleries. Plus, you'd be connecting with all the friends and family who attend our performances. Over half our shows sold out last year. We've built a great reputation." Her enthusiasm mounted as she continued. "Maybe we could hold a special opening night reception and invite everyone to come early and tour the building."

"I still don't see how you can mix a children's theater group with professional artists."

"Then let me come to the meeting tonight and make my presentation. I'm sure you'll want to move ahead when you see how this can benefit everyone." She held her breath, praying he would agree.

Crossing his arms, he studied her for a few more nerve-racking seconds.

She maintained eye contact though she could feel her left eye-lid begin to twitch.

Finally, he blew out a deep breath. "All right. You can come to the meeting. But I'm not promising you anything."

Triumph pulsed through her, and she could barely keep from pumping her fist in the air and shouting, "Yes!"

∽

CAM PACED across the shop to the window. Leaning on the counter covering the radiator, he watched Rachel Clark stride toward the parking lot, her dark brown hair swishing against her shoulders. She had spunk and determination. He could see it the tilt of her chin and hear it in her persuasive pleas. And those big brown eyes of hers could melt any guy's heart.

But he couldn't let that get to him. No way. He wouldn't let a pack of wild kids take over the building and jeopardize his business. Hopefully the rest of his friends in the co-op would agree. But after spending just a few minutes with Rachel, he suspected she would spin her story in a way that made him look like a hardhearted jerk if he said no to her proposal. Well, that was too bad. He had to do what was best for the co-op, even if he ended up looking like the bad guy.

Kids were okay. He could tolerate them, but he liked to keep his distance.

The only exception was his niece, Kayla. She was fourteen going on twenty and as cute as they come. Ever since she was a preschooler she'd had a hold on his heart he couldn't explain. He grinned at the memory of her laughing blue eyes, upturned nose, and blond curls so much like his own. Though he only saw her two or three times a year, she e-mailed him often with funny stories, photos, and updates on her life.

He responded about half the time, something that niggled his conscience.

He pushed thoughts of Kayla aside. Having an email relationship with his niece was one thing—interacting with a whole group of kids every day was another.

It had taken four years to distance himself from the painful experiences that had altered his life. He didn't want to rub those wounds raw again. For his own sanity he couldn't.

Focusing out the window once more, he watched Rachel climb into a white Toyota that looked like it had seen too many miles down the freeway. She glanced back at the building, and even at a distance he could see the longing on her face.

He clamped his jaw against his softening resolve and stepped back from the window. He wasn't going to destroy his dreams just for a pair of pretty brown eyes.

He'd be voting against Rachel Clark tonight, and if he had his way, so would everyone else.

∾

FOR MORE INFORMATION about the Bayside Treasures Series and to order your copy of SEEKING HIS LOVE visit my website: http://carrieturansky.com/index.php/books/